The Secret Files of Barry Allen

PROPERTY OF
THE FLASH

S.T.A.R.
LABORATORIES

My name is Barry Allen.

I'm the Fastest Man Alive. You probably know me by my other name as Central City's guardian speedster. They call me *THE FLASH!*

My world moves at speeds I never originally thought possible. Friends can turn to enemies, enemies to allies. Entire timelines have been rewritten in a single moment.

Even for someone like me who can puncture the sound barrier without even breaking a sweat, it can be hard to keep up. So that's why I'm writing this book. It's a collection of my greatest cases, information on my closest allies and most dangerous enemies. But most importantly, collecting all this information in one place is a way for me to finally slow down and take it all in. This book is a way for me to realize that my life is a marathon, and not a sprint.

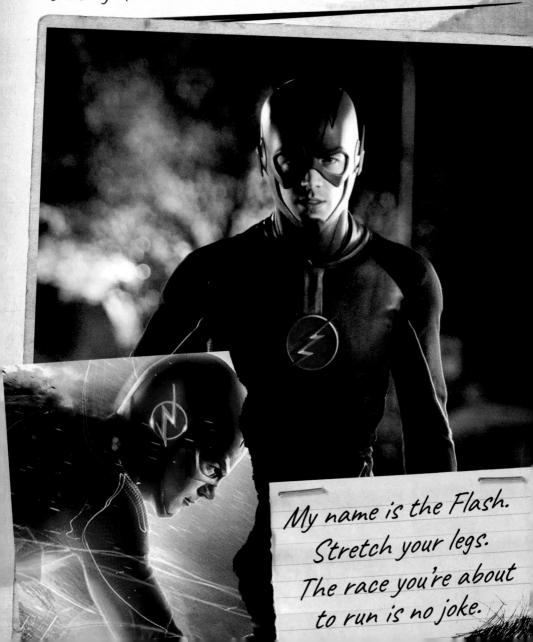

My name is the Flash.
Stretch your legs.
The race you're about
to run is no joke.

My life started out pretty normal.

I lived out in the suburbs with my mom and dad. I was always running, but back then it wasn't by choice. I was running from bullies. (I was really into science. You can imagine how popular that made me.)

That's not to say I had a bad life by any means. I wouldn't have traded it for the world.

SO_2

NH

Me and Mom

Mom always had a way of making things better. I'd come home, bruised and beaten, feeling like a loser. She'd build me right back up again, proud of me for my "good heart." Proud of me for standing up for guys smaller than me. Of course, I'm still wondering how I managed to find guys smaller than me in the first place . . .

Singin' in the Rain

Don't know how many times I watched it with mom. Somehow it never got old. I always liked how every problem in musicals got wrapped up before the final credits.

·MOM·

My dad

Henry Allen. He taught me a lot of things during our time together. Strangely, he'd teach me even more when we were forced apart.

Visiting Dad

CENTRAL CITY POLICE

DOCTOR ACCUSE
NORA ALLEN DIES

A WOMAN WELL THOUGHT OF IN HER COMMUNITY IS KILLED IN WHAT POLICE ARE CALLING "AN UNFORTUNATE DOMESTIC DISPUTE"

By Evan Gibson
Staff News Reporter, City Desk

In an event that has shocked a normally sleepy neighborhood, Nora Allen has been brutally murdered, allegedly by her husband, Dr. Henry Allen, a beloved local physician and member of the community, involved with several charitable foundations. His wife, Nora, was a real estate agent, and the mother to their young son, Barry. Before the night of the incident, the Allen household had no record of domestic disputes, a fact corroborated by countless neighbors and friends of the family.

The incident took place late in the evening when Barry was woken up by the sounds of a struggle from downstairs. While it is unclear what the boy witnessed, his mother was found with a knife wound through her chest, the murder weapon covered in Dr. Allen's fingerprints.

After being interviewed by detectives from the 52nd Division of the Central City Police Department, the boy still believed his father's innocence. However, his account of what happened that night has been dismissed by the detectives on the case, citing that the child is under immense stress and all the evidence points to Henry Allen being the only other person in the house at the time of the grisly murder. Jury selection begins next week. Barry Allen has been placed with social services for the time being.

While no one believed the story of a scared little boy, I saw what happened that night. A man—seemingly inside a ball of a yellow and red lightning—shot around our house, terrorizing my mother. Before I could do anything, the blur ran me out into the street.

OF KILLING WIFE

Police response was "almost immediate."

By the time I got home, the lightning man had killed my mother, and the police were dragging my father away, blaming him for the crime. In a flash, my entire life had turned upside down.

ALIAS
No known alias

ABILITIES
Highly trained police officer and detective with advanced hand-to-hand combat skills; proficient marksman; access to many members of the metahuman community

HOMEWORLD/DIMENSION
Earth-1

WEAKNESSES
Susceptible to conventional attacks; prioritizes family above all other loyalties

NAME

JOE WEST

Central City Police Detective Joe West took me in. As my dad's best friend, Joe believed it was his responsibility to raise me as his own. It took me years to realize it, but I was so lucky to have Joe in my life. Not to mention his daughter, Iris West.

Joe

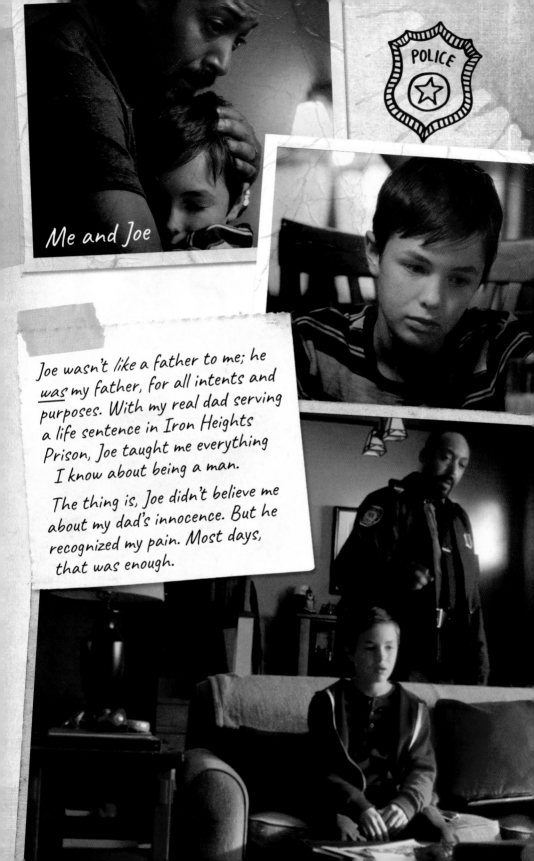

Me and Joe

Joe wasn't *like* a father to me; he was my father, for all intents and purposes. With my real dad serving a life sentence in Iron Heights Prison, Joe taught me everything I know about being a man.

The thing is, Joe didn't believe me about my dad's innocence. But he recognized my pain. Most days, that was enough.

POLICE

ALIAS
No known alias

ABILITIES
Near-fearless reporter; highly intelligent and organized; a natural born leader; trained in hand-to-hand combat and marksmanship by her police detective father; close access to many members of the metahuman community

HOMEWORLD/DIMENSION
Earth-1

WEAKNESSES
Susceptible to conventional attacks; often targeted due to her close associations with prominent metahumans

NAME
IRIS WEST

I had a crush on Iris West long before I ever went to live with her. Under different circumstances, I would have jumped at the chance to spend that much time with the girl of my dreams. As it was, I had a hard enough time just getting out of bed in the morning to face the day.

Iris made things easier, though. She didn't really know what I was going through, but she was there for me from the start. In no time, she became my best friend in the world.

Every kid has growing pains. Mine had a name. Tony Woodward, the school bully.

No matter what, Joe wasn't about to let me become a lifelong victim. He taught me how to fight back in life, both with my words and, when need be, my fists.

When I was old enough, I took a job as a forensic scientist for the Central City Police Department. I wasn't just following in the cop footsteps of Joe; I was also determined to use my training and the CCPD's resources to prove the innocence of my father, once and for all.

CENTRAL CITY POLICE
CSI
Crime Scene Investigator
NAME: BARRY ALLEN
DIV: CSI   PN: I-1E834
SIG:
CENTRAL CITY POLICE
I-1E877

STR

ALIAS
No known alias

ABILITIES
Police detective highly trained in hand-to-hand combat and marksmanship; close access to many members of the metahuman community

HOMEWORLD/DIMENSION
Earth-1

WEAKNESSES
Susceptible to conventional attacks; often targeted due to family connection to the Reverse-Flash

NAME
EDDIE THAWNE

Detective Eddie Thawne. Eddie was Joe's partner, and although it took a while, the two of us eventually became good friends. Which is pretty impressive when you think of all the things that came between us.
But more on that later.

POLICE

I can't say that Captain Singh and I are the best of friends, but as bosses go, he's not so bad. Sure, he spends more time being annoyed with me than happy that I'm doing my job, but no relationship is perfect . . .

STR

ALIAS
No known alias

ABILITIES
Highly trained police captain; very intelligent and proficient at his job; trained in hand-to-hand combat and marksmanship

HOMEWORLD/DIMENSION
Earth-1

WEAKNESSES
Susceptible to conventional attacks

NAME

CAPTAIN DAVID SINGH

Detective Ralph Dibny. He wasn't with the department long. Can't say I was a big fan of him when he was.

I'm lucky enough to get to work with Joe on the majority of my cases. With my tendency to be late for everything, Joe is always quick to offer up excuses to Captain Singh.

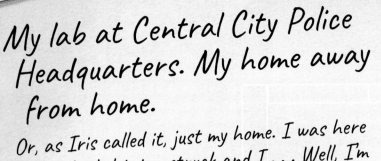

My lab at Central City Police Headquarters. My home away from home.

Or, as Iris called it, just my home. I was here the night lightning struck and I . . . Well, I'm getting ahead of myself. I'll get to that part. (It's worth the wait, believe me.)

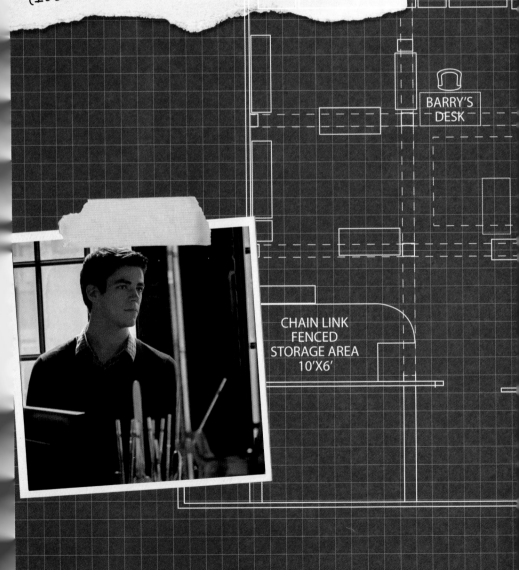

BARRY'S DESK

CHAIN LINK FENCED STORAGE AREA 10'X6'

CHAIN LINK
FENCED
STORAGE AREA
8'X11'

1/8" - 1'

Everything I knew
about the night my
mother died.

ALIAS
Oliver Queen • Arrow

POWERS/ABILITIES
Expertly trained archer with precise accuracy; trained in various martial arts and weapons techniques; in peak human condition with a grueling workout routine and diet; heir to the Queen fortune; many connections in the business, political, and superhero worlds; works with Team Arrow, a group of highly efficient crime-fighting professionals

HOMEWORLD/DIMENSION
Earth-1

WEAKNESSES
Can be susceptible to advanced martial arts–based attacks and metahuman attacks under the right conditions

NAME
GREEN ARROW

Before my life completely spiraled into crazy town, I took an unauthorized "work" trip to a town called Starling City. (It has since dropped the "ling." Star City is a lot catchier, I gotta admit.) A case revolving around a super-strong human had caught my attention, as had every bizarre and unexplained case since my mother's death.

There I was lucky enough to work on a case with the Arrow, a mysterious hooded crime fighter. I found out that the Arrow was really billionaire Oliver Queen and was able to help him while he fought a weird super-strong bad guy named Cyrus Gold. The trip didn't get me any closer to finding the secret to my mother's death, or to the strange circumstances that surrounded it. I only fanboyed out over the Arrow like five or six times. So I consider that a win.

Cyrus Gold. A thief caught stealing a Kord Centrifuge. Listen, I get it, buddy. Centrifuges are awesome. But there are other ways to go about it . . .

Turns out I was able to save Oliver Queen's life with the help of some rat poison, which in a pinch can double as a blood thinner. (Kids and sidekicks: don't try this at home.)

For some reason, Oliver thought a hood and some grease paint was enough to hide his identity from the world. So I took it upon myself to make him a mask, sort of like a parting gift.

Right away, the mask worked wonders: it actually made the Arrow smile.

I would've liked to stay longer in Starling City, but I had to get back. Harrison Wells, a personal scientific hero of mine, was about to power up the STAR Labs particle accelerator for the first time.

STR

ALIAS

██████████████

ABILITIES

Genius-level intellect; possesses scientific knowledge seemingly far beyond his years; runs STAR Labs, with access to highly advantaged technology and other genius-level employees

HOMEWORLD/DIMENSION

Earth-1

WEAKNESSES

Seemingly susceptible to conventional attacks

NAME

DR. HARRISON WELLS

To most people, it wasn't that big a deal. I mean, yeah, it made the news and everything, but most people heard about the accelerator powering up, shrugged, and went back to their regularly scheduled programming.

But to a science guy like me? It was my Super Bowl, Olympics, and the World Series all rolled up into one.

S.T.A.R. LABORATORIES

SCIENTIFIC AND TECHNOLOGICAL ADVANCED RESEARCH

A BETTER WORLD THROUGH SCIENCE

INSIDE
The Particle Accelerator

A Marvel of Modern Technology!

The Changing Face of Global Power

Harrison Wells. Maybe the greatest scientific mind on the planet. I'm not saying I had a poster of him in my room growing up—but I'm not saying I didn't, either.

So this is where things get hairy. Not gorilla hairy. (I'll get to that part. Seriously.) No, this was just your regular, run-of-the mill, near-death experience, life-changing superpowers kind of hairy.

NOTE TO SELF:
When it seems like there's more to a situation than meets the eye—there probably is.

Hey Barry,
I'm writing this to you in case you wake up while I'm gone. I've been here for way too many hours, and Dad says I need to go home and get some rest. Maybe even do some human things like take a shower or eat something. Come back to us, Barry. So much has happened since you . . . since you went to sleep. I know it sounds selfish, but I need my best friend. I miss you.

Iris

As it turned out, there was a problem during the Particle Accelerator launch. The machine overloaded, and a wave of dark-matter energy surged through all of Central City.

I was working in my lab late that night when a bolt of dark-matter-charged lightning struck not just me but also a shelf full of volatile chemicals.

I didn't die, but I didn't wake up, either. At least, not for nine months.

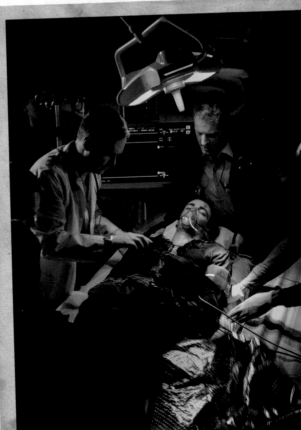

While I was in my coma, Harrison Wells and his associates at STAR Labs had me moved to their facility. Wells had convinced Joe that only they had the technology to help any possible recovery. So when I finally did wake up after nine months, the staff at STAR Labs were the first people I saw.

S.T.A.R. LABORATORIES

SUBJECT: BARRY ALLEN

ATTENDING PHYSICIAN: DR. CAITLIN SNOW

RE: PHYSICAL CONDITION UPDATE

ANALYSIS:

None of us were expecting this. I had my suspicions, with his heartbeat pulsing so fast that it couldn't be monitored on a traditional EKG. But this is like nothing I've ever seen before. Let's be clear, this is like nothing ANYONE has ever seen before.

Barry's body is in prime physical condition. Better than that, it's in a chronic and unexplained state of cellular generation. Despite being bedridden for over 270 days, his body shows no sign of deterioration or atrophy from lack of use. It's almost as if he's operating on par with a highly efficient machine, processing every calorie, every nutrient, even every breath of oxygen to its fullest extent.

That brings me to his speed. Or should I call it super-speed? There's not nearly enough room to write about it here. I'm going to need some time to figure it all out. For now, let's just say it's not a matter of applying science to Barry Allen's condition. It's a matter of science catching up with him.

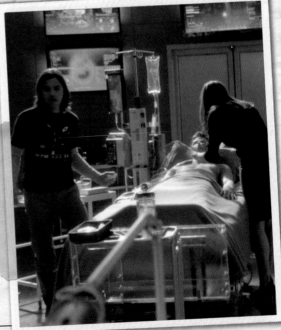

So lightning gave me abs. (Yes, you read that correctly.)

ALIAS

ABILITIES

Genius-level intellect; expert surgeon with advanced knowledge of human physiology and biology; access to highly advanced technology at STAR Labs; connections to Mercury Labs; well-respected among the metahuman and scientific communities

HOMEWORLD/DIMENSION

Earth-1

WEAKNESSES

Seemingly susceptible to conventional attacks

NAME

DR. CAITLIN SNOW

Although she seemed a little distant, and maybe cold at first, Caitlin was a huge help when it came down to determining what my body could do after the accident. I think she was even more surprised than me.

Caitlin's fiancé, Ronnie Raymond. He was caught in the particle accelerator explosion and was presumed dead. But in reality, the situation was way crazier.

Somehow, the particle accelerator explosion had changed my very DNA. I was a metahuman now, capable of moving at speeds unheard of for a human being.

STAR LABORATORIES

SUBJECT: BARRY ALLEN

EXPERIMENT NO. 101-THE SUPERSPEED TRIALS!

ANALYSIS:

Oh man, is this dude fast! I'm not kidding around here. This guy lit up the track at the Ferris Air Testing Facility. Seriously. I'm surprised there weren't flames coming off of his feet. (Were there flames? I need to rewind the feed and see.)

Okay, so what do we know? We know Barry has broken any and all track-and-field records on his first time out on the runway. That's not even in question. The guy passed 200 miles per hour in nothing flat!

We know he's creating a ton of friction, but he doesn't even seem to feel it. Is he tapping into some other outside force? Some sort of energy field or realm we don't yet know about?

We also know that he needs to learn how to put on the brakes a little. Guy's fast, but he's not too coordinated just yet.

Good thing is, we also know he can heal right up. His metabolism is incredibly advanced. He shook off a broken arm in three hours. <u>THREE HOURS!</u>

Okay, so that's what we know so far. Oh yeah, and one more thing. We know my job here at STAR Labs is going to be anything but boring for the foreseeable future.

Cisco had no idea how right he was.

ALIAS

███████████████

ABILITIES

Genius-level intellect; inventor and mechanical expert; brilliant computer programmer and engineer; access to highly advanced technology at STAR Labs; well-connected among the metahuman and scientific communities

HOMEWORLD/DIMENSION

Earth-1

WEAKNESSES

Seemingly susceptible to conventional attacks

NAME

FRANCISCO "CISCO" RAMON

In addition to being a genius, Cisco has a real knack for naming metahumans.

We started out as work friends. These days, he's like a brother to me. A brother who's also a really bad influence.

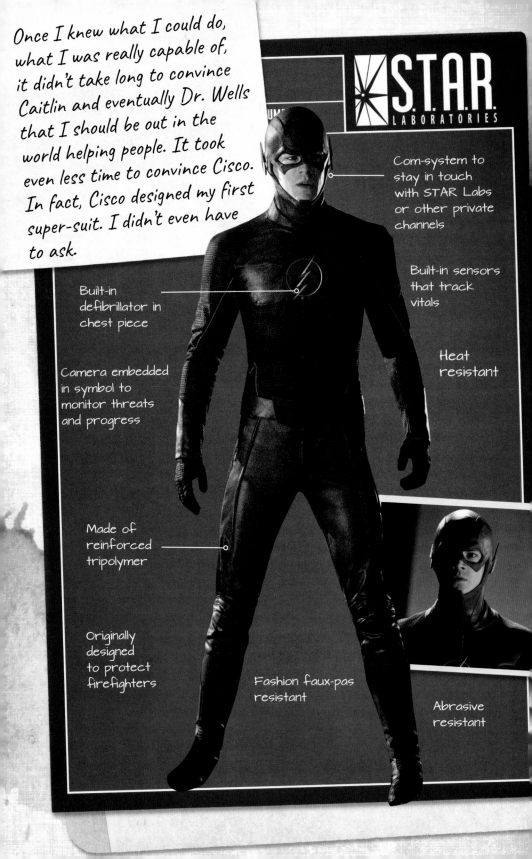

Once I knew what I could do, what I was really capable of, it didn't take long to convince Caitlin and eventually Dr. Wells that I should be out in the world helping people. It took even less time to convince Cisco. In fact, Cisco designed my first super-suit. I didn't even have to ask.

S.T.A.R. LABORATORIES

Com-system to stay in touch with STAR Labs or other private channels

Built-in sensors that track vitals

Heat resistant

Built-in defibrillator in chest piece

Camera embedded in symbol to monitor threats and progress

Made of reinforced tripolymer

Originally designed to protect firefighters

Fashion faux-pas resistant

Abrasive resistant

My foray into the world of crime fighting was a team effort from the start. Dr. Wells, Cisco, and Caitlin were my eyes and ears back at STAR Labs, always whispering to me and pooling their knowledge to get me out of some of the strangest situations you can imagine.

Becoming a superhero meant getting an entirely new outlook on life. Rogue metahumans too tough for the police to deal with suddenly became my responsibility. The first was Clyde Mardon, a killer who received superpowers when his plane was caught in the dark-matter wave from the particle accelerator explosion.

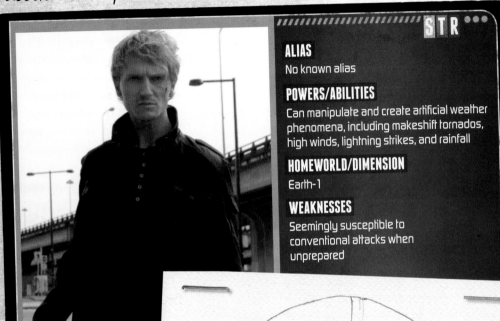

STR

ALIAS
No known alias

POWERS/ABILITIES
Can manipulate and create artificial weather phenomena, including makeshift tornados, high winds, lightning strikes, and rainfall

HOMEWORLD/DIMENSION
Earth-1

WEAKNESSES
Seemingly susceptible to conventional attacks when unprepared

NAME
CLYDE MARDON

A police sketch artist's drawing of Mardon based on witness testimony. Proof that Mardon survived the dark-matter wave.

CENTRAL CITY POLICE DEPARTME
EVIDENCE:

Still from a security camera at Gold City Bank. Witnesses described a storm inside the building similar to a hurricane.

CENTRAL CITY POLICE

3·1·2·6·1·8·7·4·1·7

After I stopped Mardon's tornado, he had me in his sights. I was too spent to act, but thankfully Joe West was there. He shot and killed Mardon, and in the process, he saw me without my mask.

It took some time for Joe to adjust to my secret, but looking back on it, I couldn't have asked for a better partner on the inside.

Becoming a superhero isn't exactly easy. There are plenty of bumps in the road to deal with. My first major issue came when I started experiencing dizzy spells after using my speed. Thanks to Caitlin's diagnosis and Cisco's "Cosmic Treadmill," we soon discovered that my new biology requires lots and lots of calories. Luckily, that's why the universe made Big Belly Burger.

ITEM COSMIC TREADMILL

SCHEMATIC Cisco Ramon **NUMBER** 008

S.T.A.R.
LABORATORIES

Most home treadmills have a maximum speed of about 12 miles per hour. This baby has personally received the Cisco treatment, and can handle whatever Barry can dish out. At least I hope so.

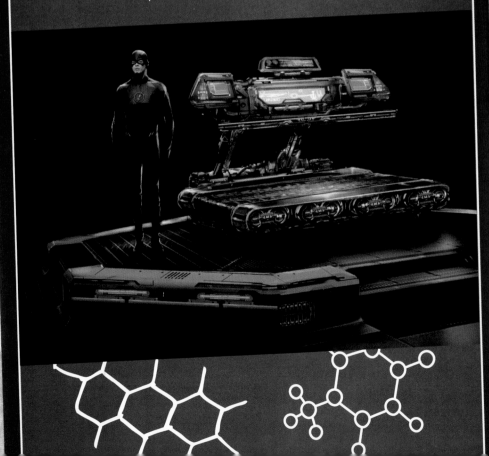

When I don't have time (or money) to order thirteen #4s with extra cheese, I have these high-calorie protein bars that Cisco specially designed for me. Delicious? No. Dry and flavorless? Yes and yes.

Becoming a superhero meant my main priority was to take down other metahumans. I just didn't think there would be so many of them!

ALIAS
Danton Black

POWERS/ABILITIES
Able to multiply his form into dozens of near-exact copies, all controlled by the original

HOMEWORLD/DIMENSION
Earth-1

WEAKNESSES
Can be defeated by targeting the original body

Transformed into a one-man army by the STAR Labs explosion, Multiplex wanted nothing more than the death of his employer, industrialist Simon Stagg.

NAME

MULITPLEX

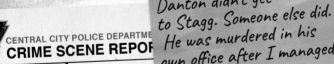

Danton didn't get to Stagg. Someone else did. He was murdered in his own office after I managed to stop Multiplex.

 CENTRAL CITY POLICE DEPARTME...
CRIME SCENE REPOR...

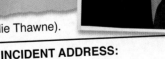

CASE NO	#SE1EP2	
REPORTING OFFICER	Barry Allen (after Detectives Joe West and Eddie Thawne).	
VICTIM INFORMATION	**NAME:** - Tony Albano - Owner, Hex's Gun Shop	**INCIDENT ADDRESS:** - 10 All-Star Avenue - Central City
DESCRIPTION OF CRIME SCENE	**POSITION OF VICTIM:** - Facedown on shop floor near broken glass of a display case. - Bullet wound in victim indicates small caliber handgun. **STOLEN ITEMS:** - Glock 19s. Six, perhaps more. - Each fitted with extra ammunition magazines. **DETAILS OF EVENT:** - While security camera footage shows only one perp, footprints at scene reveal six suspects, each wearing identical size 10 shoes. - Awaiting coroner's findings for exact time of death and confirmation of cause of death.	

CONFIDENTIAL

ALIAS
Kyle Nimbus

POWERS/ABILITIES
Can turn his entire body into poison gas;
many mafia connections

HOMEWORLD/DIMENSION
Earth-1

WEAKNESSES
When caught overtaxing his powers,
he becomes solid and vulnerable to
conventional attacks

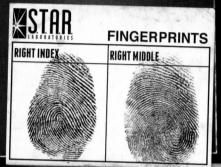

S.T.A.R. LABORATORIES
FINGERPRINTS

RIGHT INDEX	RIGHT MIDDLE

NAME
THE MIST

The Mist targeted mob bosses throughout Central City, including members of the Darbinyan crime family.

It soon became clear that the Mist was targeting those he perceived as having wronged him in the past, targets ranging from that crime family to a judge, to the lead detective who brought him down: Joe West.

It took a little patience and a lot of speed, but I was finally able to stop the Mist before he could murder Joe or anyone else. The only problem was, Iron Heights Prison wasn't equipped for metahumans like him. So we had to improvise . . .

CINEMA TICKET

THE VOGUE THEATER
CENTRAL CITY

BLUE DEVIL II: HELL TO PAY

RATED R $10.97
FRI 7:00PM · HOUSE: 10   GENAD WEEKEND

Saw this with Iris the night the Mist first attacked. Not a bad popcorn flick, but only a 4 on the zombie movie scale. Probably should have gone to _The Rita Farr Story_ instead.

Cisco came up with the idea. We already had a facility perfect for shielding extreme power from the populace: the STAR Labs particle accelerator itself. If a standard jail cell couldn't hold a metahuman, we'd make one that would. The Pipeline.

Anti-proton cavities in the reactor are the perfect size for containing individual prisoners

Barrier is powered by an 8.3 Tesla super-conducting electromagnet which is about 100,000 times the strength of Earth's magnetic field

Makeshift prison located below main hub, allowing easy access and monitoring capabilities for the STAR Labs staff

Ideally, holding facility will be temporary, buying us time to determine how to remove each prisoner's powers permanently.

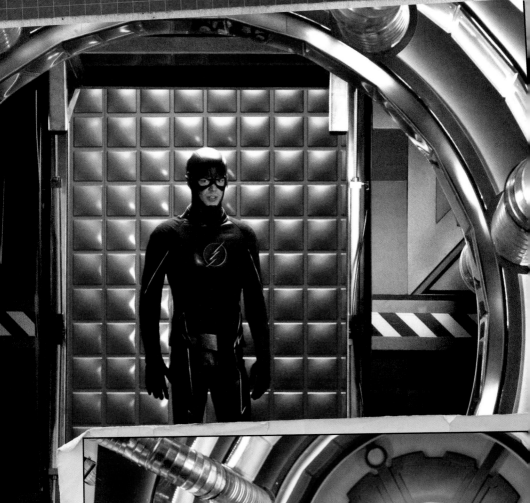

Most of Central City's criminals are amateurs. Guys who stumbled into powers by accident (like me!), with no real grasp of how to apply them (also like me). But every now and then, you get someone like Leonard Snart. Snart was cool under pressure even before he got his Cold Gun. Every crime was planned out to the second. So when Central City gained its own resident crime fighter, Snart knew I was the x-factor he had to remove from the equation.

ALIAS
Leonard Snart

POWERS/ABILITIES
Master planner; extremely well-connected in both the criminal underworld and metahuman communities; operates stolen STAR Labs hi-tech Cold Gun capable of instantly freezing its targets; member of the superhero team Legends with access to their advanced technology

HOMEWORLD/DIMENSION
Earth-1

WEAKNESSES
Susceptible to conventional attacks when unarmed; has a weak spot for his sister, Golden Glider

NAME
CAPTAIN COLD

The Cold Gun is one of Cisco's inventions. It was stolen from STAR Labs back when the lab was guarded only by a skeleton crew. If he had told me he had a fail-safe in place in case I ever got out of hand, that would be one thing. But he didn't, and so my first bout with Captain Cold went as bad as could be expected. Someone died because our team didn't communicate.

Still needs a little tweaking but I'm basically done with this bad boy. I give you, Cisco Ramon's patent-pending Cold Gun! Yeah, maybe the name needs work, but I'm gonna let this thing speak for itself.

Handheld compact cryo-engine

Powered by a microcomputer that regulates air-to-fuel ratio

Built to achieve absolute zero instantly

Perfect for stopping a speedster in his tracks if need be

Needs goggles to safely operate. That glare is no joke!

Eager to prove himself, Cisco tracked the Cold Gun via its update software, and even stopped Cold from killing me by tricking him into thinking the STAR Labs vacuum cleaner was some sort of hi-tech gun.

MUSEUM

KAHNDAQ DYNASTY

DIAMOND EXHIBIT

TREASURES UNEARTHED FROM THE DAYS OF ADAM

A limited engagement

Only Leonard Snart would make a play for a diamond exhibit with more security than the White House. Luckily, Joe West spotted him taking the tour, and was able to chase him off.

CENTRAL CITY

Like it or not, Cold became a regular fixture in my so-called Rogues Gallery. While he was one of my most dedicated enemies, he also operated by a code of ethics. For instance, when he later learned my secret identity, Cold kept it to himself—for a price. The only time you ever had to worry about Cold was when he wasn't trying to make a profit.

Say goodbye to your Central City Police Department's standard-issue ballistic shield. And say hello to the new-and-improved Ciscoed model!

Lined with a pretty sweet compacted heating ribbon

Specifically designed to repel temperature attacks, especially those reaching absolute zero

So basically, Captain Cold is out of luck.

Tell your friends!

In an effort to win back some of the goodwill they lost during the particle accelerator incident, Dr. Wells and Cisco worked with the CCPD to help arm their men against a Captain Cold-specific attack.

STR •••

ALIAS
Felicity Smoak

ABILITIES
Genius-level intellect; highly connected in the metahuman and business worlds; expert computer hacker and engineer; quick-witted and resourceful on her feet; trained in hand-to-hand combat by Green Arrow

HOMEWORLD/DIMENSION
Earth-1

WEAKNESSES
Susceptible to conventional attacks; weak spot for the safety of Oliver Queen

NAME

OVERWATCH

Sometimes you wonder how things would have ended up if your life were just a little bit different. Felicity Smoak is a perfect example of right person, wrong time.

When I first visited Starling City, Felicity and I instantly hit it off. It was her idea to involve me when the Arrow was on his deathbed, and she visited me in Central City after I gained my speed. We even tried our hand at dating—sort of. I think it would've worked out, if I wasn't in love with someone else and if she wasn't in love with someone else. But besides those tiny little details, we were perfect together.

I could geek out with Felicity all day long about nuclear fission, but in the end, can that really compare to a guy who does pull-ups for fun? FOR. FUN.

If I had a dollar for every time I got a coffee at C.C. Jitters, I'd... well, I'd still be severely in the hole, funds-wise. It's not the cheapest coffee bar in Central City, but since Iris got a job there, it's become our usual hangout spot—when I can catch a minute or two away from STAR Labs. They also throw a pretty mean trivia night. Watch out for team E=MC Hammer. We're a force to be reckoned with.

c c j i t t e r s

Don't get the idea that everyone caught in the particle accelerator explosion turned into evil criminal geniuses. Some, like Plastique, were misguided, just lashing out after their worlds were turned upside down.

STR

ALIAS
Bette Sans Souci

POWERS/ABILITIES
Can turn anything she touches into an explosive; explosive device expert; advanced military training

HOMEWORLD/DIMENSION
Earth-1

WEAKNESSES
Susceptible to conventional attacks when unprepared

NAME
PLASTIQUE

CENTRAL CITY
POLICE

CENTRAL CITY POLICE DEPARTMENT
EVIDENCE:_____

General Eiling is not what you'd call a shining example of Army pride. The guy is unscrupulous at best, corrupt at worst. While he didn't create Plastique, he certainly viewed her as a weapon rather than a human being.

STR

ALIAS
No known alias

ABILITIES
Military general with high-ranking connections in politics and government; skilled soldier and marksman; access to soldiers and military weaponry

HOMEWORLD/DIMENSION
Earth-1

WEAKNESSES
Susceptible to conventional attacks

NAME
GENERAL EILING

Plastique confronted Eiling and was shot and killed during their fight, forcing me to run her out onto the water when she self-destructed.

CENTRAL CITY POLICE DEPARTMEN
EVIDENCE:

Eiling covered up the explosion, saying it was a routine underwater weapons' test. And just like that, the real bad guy got away with it.

EXPLOSION IN RIVER   CHANNEL 52
NEWS REPORT

Every kid fantasizes about getting super powers— whether it's to fly, turn invisible, or be faster than a speeding bullet. I think it's because we're all so powerless when we're young. We want a way to stand on equal footing with the grown-ups, or at the very least, stand up to that mean kid in class.

STR

ALIAS
Tony Woodward

POWERS/ABILITIES
Able to turn his entire body or parts of his body into metal; superhuman strength, durability, and endurance

HOMEWORLD/DIMENSION
Earth-1

WEAKNESSES
Susceptible to a "super-sonic punch"

NAME
GIRDER

So you'd think that when I actually achieved that one-in-a-million dream of having super powers, I wouldn't still be getting trounced by my high school bully. You'd think that, but you'd be wrong.

My childhood bully, Tony Woodward, had been turned into Girder, a man who could transform into metal at a moment's notice. When we first fought, he was stealing a Humvee loaded with Rusty Iron Brewing kegs. That led Eddie Thawne and me right to one of his buddies who told us Tony's story. During the particle accelerator incident, Tony fell into a vat of molten scrap at Keystone Ironworks. As luck would have it, my former bully was made into an actual man of steel.

  When Tony kidnapped Iris and took her to Carmichael Elementary, our old school, I got another shot at Girder. By running over five miles to gain up enough speed, I was able to deliver a "super-sonic punch," as Cisco called it. While it could have crushed every bone in my body, it broke through Girder's metal form instead, and we were soon able to fit him with his own holding cell at STAR Labs.

Even after he was killed, Girder made his way back in zombie form. He was the bully that just wouldn't die.

ALIAS
Bartholomew Henry "Barry" Allen •
The Streak (unofficial)

POWERS/ABILITIES
Can move at superhuman speeds; super-fast
healing; able to create tornados or other
cyclones by moving his limbs at super-speed;
can vibrate through solid objects; able to
increase the speed in others; able to run so
fast he can go back or forward in time;
genius-level intellect; highly trained police
forensic scientist; access to the geniuses at
STAR Labs as well as that institution's vast
array of scientific equipment and weaponry

HOMEWORLD/DIMENSION
Earth-1

WEAKNESSES
Standard human strength and durability
makes him susceptible to a wide variety
of attacks when unprepared; will do almost
anything to save his friends and family;
vulnerable to Time Wraiths like any
speedster

NAME
THE FLASH

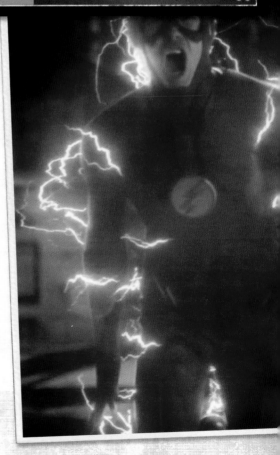

I should know by now that
when Iris gets an idea, there's
no talking her out of it. But
when she started to blog
about the strange "Streak"
running around Central
City, stopping bad guys at
super-speed, I did my best to
warn her of the dangers of
connecting herself
to the city's new hero.

   The only advice she actually
took was to change the name
from the Streak to the Flash.

   Yeah, I know. The Arrow
thought of "the Flash" first.
But I'm gonna take this as a
personal victory anyway.

Iris's blog went from a cult fascination to the go-to news source for all things Flash. Great for her career as an aspiring writer and a fed-up barista. Bad for her safety and Joe's blood pressure level.

SAVED BY THE FLASH!

By Iris West

To understand what I'm about to tell you, you need to do something first, you need to believe in the impossible. Can you do that? Good. Because all of us, we've forgotten what miracles look like. Maybe because they haven't made much of an appearance lately. Our lives have become ordinary.

But there is someone out there who is truly extraordinary. I don't know where you came from. I don't know your name. But I have seen you do the impossible to protect the city I love.

So for those of us who believe in you and what you're doing, I just want to say thank you.

Today I was saved by the impossible. A mystery man. The Fastest Man Alive. Then a friend gave me an idea for a new name. And something tells me, it's going to catch on.

Barry, you talk some sense into her, or I'm going to knock some sense into you.
—Joe

I think this is what they call "tough love."

It's bad enough dealing with a city full of hometown super-villains. But when I have to start fighting other heroes' bad guys, that's just unfair. Good thing I have my own "super team" for just that type of emergency. And by "super team," I mean the tough-as-nails West family.

STR

ALIAS
William Tockman

POWERS/ABILITIES
Master planner obsessed with things running like clockwork; computer and hacking expert; expert marksman

HOMEWORLD/DIMENSION
Earth-1

WEAKNESSES
Susceptible to conventional attacks

NAME
CLOCK KING

Clock King was a particularly OCD villain who originally clashed with the Arrow.
So of course he waited to cause more trouble until he was at our Central City Police Department. There, he stole a gun, quickly creating a hostage situation.

Luckily for all those well-trained cops, Iris West was one of the captives. She managed to get to Eddie's ankle holster and hold Tockman at gunpoint until he was safely in police custody once again.

Just like clockwork.

Sorry, I couldn't resist. Caitlin says I have a problem.

ALIAS
Farooq Gibran

POWERS/ABILITIES
Can absorb and redirect electricity in the form of lightning bolts; able to absorb Flash's speed force energy

HOMEWORLD/DIMENSION
Earth-1

WEAKNESSES
Forced to feed off electricity often; too much energy absorption can overload system

Dubbed "Blackout" by Cisco, Farooq Gibran was climbing an electric tower the night of the particle accelerator explosion.

NAME
BLACKOUT

When I first met him, Blackout siphoned off my powers, temporarily reducing me to normal human speed. Let me tell you, if you're used to super-speed, not having it is like running through a pool of Jell-O. All day, every day.

When Blackout later attacked STAR Labs, Dr. Wells freed Girder to serve as a distraction. Blackout killed him and soon confronted Wells himself.

After my run on Cisco's "Cosmic Treadmill," seeing Harrison Wells in danger jumpstarted my powers, and I defeated Blackout when his system overloaded from siphoning off too much of my energy. It killed him.

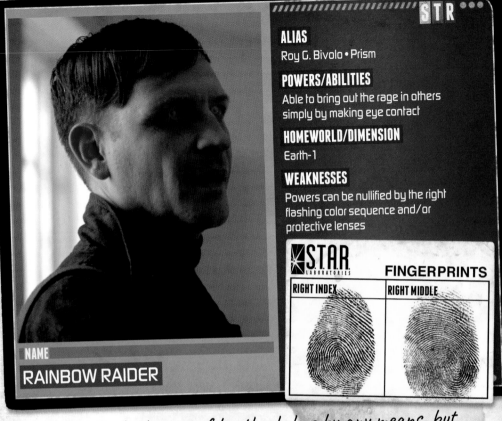

ALIAS
Roy G. Bivolo • Prism

POWERS/ABILITIES
Able to bring out the rage in others simply by making eye contact

HOMEWORLD/DIMENSION
Earth-1

WEAKNESSES
Powers can be nullified by the right flashing color sequence and/or protective lenses

S.T.A.R. LABORATORIES

FINGERPRINTS

RIGHT INDEX	RIGHT MIDDLE

NAME
RAINBOW RAIDER

Central City isn't the city of brotherly love by any means, but it's also not the sort of place where normal everyday people start punching each other at the local bank. So when that sort of thing happens, you guessed it: it's Flash time.

The perp made off with a half a million dollars when the bank became an impromptu fight club. It was the work of a metahuman, Roy G. Bivolo. And yes, before you say anything, Cisco did have a field day with that name.

STAR LABORATORIES

SUBJECT: The Powers of Prism
(Not the Rainbow Raider.)
(Because Caitlin definitely doesn't
get to make up the names.)
(Prism trademark by Cisco Ramon.)

ANALYSIS:

Let's go over what we know:

Bivolo has crazy powers—like if he makes eye contact with you and his eyes turn red, you get whammied and become angrier than a commuter on the 16 bus line.

Flash was exposed to said crazy powers.

Ergo Flash was a rage-a-holic with the power to move faster than we can think.

Wells worked up a spectrum dealy to negate the effects, but what he hasn't theorized yet is what if Prism can actually activate other colors on the emotional spectrum?

What if he turns yellow and can activate fear? Green for bravery, orange for greed? The possibilities are endless, a full emotional . . . Prism.

Again, the name just makes sense.

Thanks to Dr. Wells, the effects of Rainbow Raider's angry influence were short-lived. I was able to take the new metahuman down and imprison him at STAR Labs, but I got a little help from another colorful friend. A guy in green. Maybe you've heard of him?

Arrow showed up in Central City alongside Felicity and his partner-in-crime-fighting, John Diggle. They were on the trail of a killer Cisco named Captain Boomerang because of his weapon of choice. They helped us with the Rainbow Raider, so I took the trip to Starling City to help them with their boomerang killer.

STR

ALIAS
Digger Harkness

POWERS/ABILITIES
Expert marksman with a boomerang; highly trained in hand-to-hand combat; armed with flash smoke bombs and trick boomerangs; advanced military training; ties to the Suicide Squad as a former member; explosives and computer expert

HOMEWORLD/DIMENSION
Earth-1

WEAKNESSES
Susceptible to conventional attacks when unprepared

NAME
CAPTAIN BOOMERANG

Arrow's methods are way too extreme for my tastes, including his willingness to use torture to get information. Thanks to Arrow's tactics, Captain Boomerang was able to invade his Arrowcave and injure Lyla Michaels, Diggle's fiancée. Luckily, we stopped Boomerang and his plan to bomb Starling City. I think Arrow learned something from his brief partnership with Team Flash. And I think I learned a few things too. For instance, I learned that he hates when we call it the "Arrowcave."

ALIAS
John Diggle

POWERS/ABILITIES
Expertly trained in hand-to-hand combat and in various weapons, including the bow and arrow; expert marksman; access to Team Arrow and the resources of Oliver Queen; natural born leader with ties to the government organization ARGUS; military training; bodyguard training; wears specially designed armored suit

HOMEWORLD/DIMENSION
Earth-1

WEAKNESSES
Susceptible to conventional attacks when unprepared

NAME
SPARTAN

Arrow's friend Diggle doesn't like to be "Flashed" around places. He has a tendency to get motion sickness. He pukes. Like, a lot. It's better to let the guy provide his own transportation.

Felicity found traces of iron oxide on one of Captain Boomerang's boomerangs, inspiring Team Arrow to pay my city a visit. Central City has the largest concentration of iron oxide in the country.

ALIAS
Martin Stein and Ronnie Raymond

POWERS/ABILITIES
Flight; psychic bond between two identities when separated; able to expel and absorb nuclear energy; genius-level intellect; combined intelligence and life skills of two unique individuals; superhuman endurance and durability

HOMEWORLD/DIMENSION
Earth-1

WEAKNESSES
Strong applications of force or wind; certain radiation

NAME

FIRESTORM

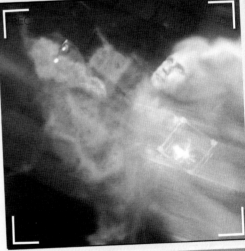

Ronnie Raymond had been a STAR Labs employee before his "death," not to mention Caitlin Snow's fiancé. When he was caught in the particle accelerator explosion, he didn't actually die. He merged forms with Dr. Martin Stein, another particle accelerator victim.

When Ronnie Raymond first emerged with super powers, Caitlin began investigating. This led her to the F.I.R.E.S.T.O.R.M. project, and to Jason Rusch, a new hire at STAR's main competitor, Mercury Labs.

Jason was working on F.I.R.E.S.T.O.R.M. with team leader Professor Martin Stein, trying to alter matter on a molecular level. He had no idea that Stein had been caught in the particle accelerator explosion, just that the army was after Stein and had confiscated his research.

Ronnie and Stein didn't have much in common, but when they were Firestorm, they were a well-oiled machine, using Stein's brains and Ronnie's physical instincts.

Best of both worlds.

CENTRAL CITY POLICE DEF
EVIDENCE:_____

The fury of Firestorm.

> Ronald, are you available?

> Prof, we share a psychic link. You know I'm not available right now.

> Well, I know you don't want to be available, yes. Although I'm not sure why.

> Let me guess, you're playing a video game about mass destruction.

> It's about stopping the world from mass destruction. Big difference.

> Yes, well, I need your assistance.

> No you don't.

> Ronald . . .

> We've got that link, remember? And it's growing way stronger now that we willingly fused ourselves.

> That doesn't mean I don't require assistance.

> I can tell it's not life or death, though. What, you want to merge so we can fly into town? You have an errand or something?

> Something.

> Gonna have to be more specific if you want me to help.

> I have a few library books in desperate need of returning. The library closes in less than five minutes, and I'm afraid I'll be facing a fine if this matter isn't resolved quickly.

> Are you kidding me right now?

> It will only take a moment. And then you can get back to destroying—

> Saving.

> Saving the world via joystick.

> You have so much to learn about modern video games.

> Tell me about it on the way to the library.

When Ronnie returned to Central City to help me out of a tight spot, he and Caitlin decided to tie the knot. Fittingly, Dr. Stein officiated.

Captain Cold wasn't just a highly organized thief. He was also well-connected in Central City's underground. After we first fought, he didn't just want to pull off another heist—he wanted revenge against me. So he started to assemble his own Rogues. The first of which was his longtime partner, Mick Rory.

ALIAS
Mick Rory

POWERS/ABILITIES
Experienced fighter with an uncouth style; utilizes stolen Heat Gun; affiliated with many other Central City Rogues; member of the superhero team Legends with access to their advanced technology

HOMEWORLD/DIMENSION
Earth-1

WEAKNESSES
Susceptible to conventional attacks when unprepared; obsession with fire can cause distraction

NAME
HEAT WAVE

Cold and Heat Wave kidnapped Caitlin to draw me out. Luckily, beating the pair was as easy as getting them to cross their streams.

Fire and Ice don't play nice together.

HEAT GUN

SCHEMATIC Cisco Ramon **NUMBER** 012

Look at this thing. It's not just me, is it? The word "primitive" comes to mind.

Okay, all style failings aside—and there are a lot of them with this design—what this gun lacks in aesthetics, it makes up in the force of its firepower.

It fires highly concentrated combustible liquid fuel.

Fuel ignites on contact with the air, creating an effect that would make any run-of-the-mill flame-thrower jealous.

There's a lot of potential for improvement here, if I can just get my hands on it. Which pretty much means someone will have to pry it from Rory's . . .

Captain Cold stole a Heat Gun the same day he stole his Cold Gun. He figured it was a perfect match for Rory, the pyromaniac. And with a new gun came a new name: Heat Wave.

CENTRAL CITY POLICE DEPARTMENT
EVIDENCE:

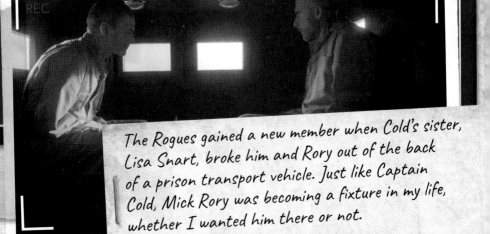

The Rogues gained a new member when Cold's sister, Lisa Snart, broke him and Rory out of the back of a prison transport vehicle. Just like Captain Cold, Mick Rory was becoming a fixture in my life, whether I wanted him there or not.

When the Flash was forced into the public eye, Iris's blog got caught in my drift. The Central City Picture News hired her as their new reporter, hoping to nab exclusive Flash stories in the bargain.

With Dr. Wells in my ear and STAR Labs' resources at Cisco's and Caitlin's fingertips, Team Flash was finally coming together. Good news for us, bad news for the city's criminals, like the Royal Flush Gang.

— Central City —
Picture News

— Central City —
Picture News

IRIS WEST
REPORTER

icture N

FLUSHED! PRESS

Iris West, cub reporter.

By Mason Bridge

CENTRAL CITY – Fresh off his fight with so-called Captain Cold, in which the public finally received confirmation that the superhero named the Flash is very much real and not an urban myth, the Scarlet Speedster raced into danger again when confronting three motorcyclist members of the Royal Flush Gang. Named after the playing cards in a standard suit,

CONTINUED ON 2A

Iris's coworker, sports writer Linda Park. We dated for a short time, but it just wasn't meant to be.

Iris started out at *Picture News* shadowing Mason Bridge. He finally warmed up to her, but somebody murdered him when he started digging into the death of Simon Stagg.

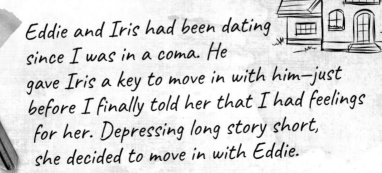

Eddie and Iris had been dating since I was in a coma. He gave Iris a key to move in with him—just before I finally told her that I had feelings for her. Depressing long story short, she decided to move in with Eddie.

ALIAS
Hartley Rathaway

POWERS/ABILITIES
Experienced fighter with an uncouth style; utilizes stolen Heat Gun; affiliated with many other Central City Rogues; member of the superhero team Legends with access to their advanced technology

HOMEWORLD/DIMENSION
Earth-1

WEAKNESSES
Susceptible to conventional attacks when unprepared; obsession with fire can cause distraction

NAME

PIED PIPER

Hartley Rathaway was Harrison Wells's right-hand man before the particle accelerator explosion. While he clashed with Cisco from the second Cisco was hired, Rathaway focused his anger on Dr. Wells when he became the Pied Piper.

Hartley was an expert chess player, and as such he planned out his moves several steps in advance. He wanted me to catch him destroying his family business so he could break out of his cell in the Pipeline and hack into STAR Labs' files. His entire plan was a revenge scheme against Harrison Wells.

ITEM: Gauntlets

SCHEMATIC: Cisco Ramon NUMBER: 103

S.T.A.R. CONFIDENTIAL LABORATORIES

A technical genius, Pied Piper designed his own sonic gauntlets to attack the family business that shunned him just because of his sexual orientation.

Apparently, Rathaway had discovered a flaw in the particle accelerator back when he worked at STAR. When he told Wells that it might explode if activated, Wells had him fired. Pied Piper used his hack on STAR to find out my vibrational frequency, and incapacitated me as soon as I confronted him. Luckily for me, Wells had my back and tuned the radios in nearby cars to a frequency that destroyed the Piper's arsenal.

A criminal named Clay Parker just up and vanished from his cell at Iron Heights Prison. That's the jail where my dad was being held, so I can tell you that's no easy accomplishment. After a little STAR Labs–style digging, we discovered our perp: Parker's girlfriend, a particle accelerator metahuman dubbed Peek-A-Boo.

STR

ALIAS
Shawna Baez

POWERS/ABILITIES
Able to teleport to any location she can see; can take others with her on her jumps

HOMEWORLD/DIMENSION
Earth-1

WEAKNESSES
Needs to be able to see where she's teleporting to

NAME

PEEK-A-BOO

Peek-A-Boo's telescope, her low-tech way of jumping further distances. Once we figured out how her jumps worked, all we had to do was shut off the lights to prevent her from teleporting. Well, that and adjust her cell in the Pipeline so that she couldn't just jump right out of it . . .

Peek-A-Boo rescued Parker by taking small jumps at a time. If she had skipped town that night, I doubt we would have found her. But Parker had racked up a lot of debt with a local criminal. He convinced Peek-A-Boo to help him pull off a few jobs before they left Central City.

Writing about the Weather Wizard should be fairly straight forward. He's the revenge-seeking brother of Clyde Mardon. They were both caught in the same accident, and both gained weather-controlling powers as a result. Pretty easy to understand, right? The only thing is, I first met the Weather Wizard in a timeline that no longer exists . . .

STR •••

ALIAS
Mark Mardon

POWERS/ABILITIES
Able to create and weaponize artificial weather, including various windstorms, hail, rain, and lightning; able to alter temperatures; can use wind manipulation to fly

HOMEWORLD/DIMENSION
Earth-1

WEAKNESSES
Wizard's Wand

 CENTRAL CITY POLICE DEPARTME
EVIDENCE:

NAME
WEATHER WIZARD

During our first clash, Weather Wizard created a tsunami large enough to drown the city. I ran so fast to stop it that I actually ran back in time. The second go-around, I did things differently, changing the timeline as a result. And I easily caged the Weather Wizard before he ever even thought of creating his massive wave.

Hi-tech version of an active lightning rod

Point it at the sky and zap!

(Well, not so much of a zap, really. More of a low hum.
But that's not nearly as dramatic . . .)

It'll absorb like a sponge whatever energy's floating around
it

Essentially, it's a rod-shaped vacuum cleaner that sucks
up atmospheric electrons, negating the Weather Wizard's
powers

Zap!

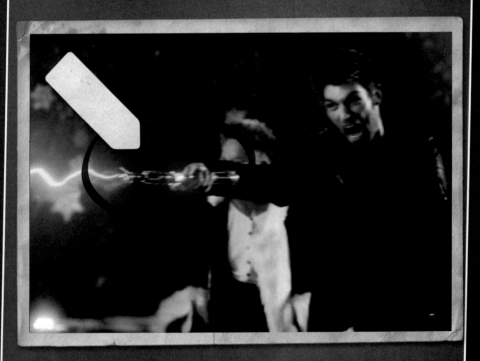

In the new reality that sprung up after I ran back in time a day, Captain Cold and Heat Wave kidnapped Cisco and his brother, Dante, in order to force Cisco to create new Heat and Cold Guns for them. But Cold's sister, Lisa, didn't want to be left out of the action. So Cisco made her a Gold Gun. Just like that, Central City got a new Rogue: the Golden Glider.

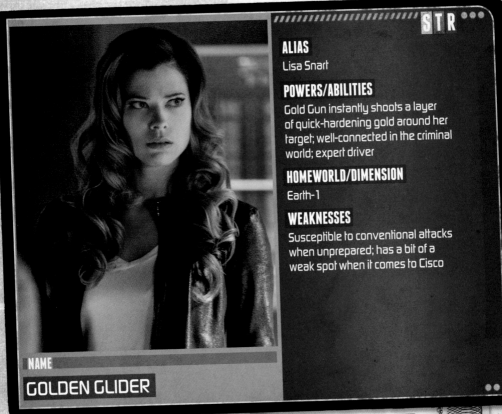

STR

ALIAS
Lisa Snart

POWERS/ABILITIES
Gold Gun instantly shoots a layer of quick-hardening gold around her target; well-connected in the criminal world; expert driver

HOMEWORLD/DIMENSION
Earth-1

WEAKNESSES
Susceptible to conventional attacks when unprepared; has a bit of a weak spot when it comes to Cisco

NAME

GOLDEN GLIDER

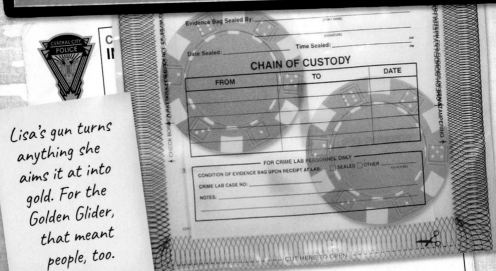

Lisa's gun turns anything she aims it at into gold. For the Golden Glider, that meant people, too.

The Gold Gun

ITEM The Gold Gun

SCHEMATIC Cisco Ramon **NUMBER** 201

Okay, so this one is a little tricky. Lisa likes gold, and I like Lisa when she's not trying to murder me. Obviously, I can't create a weapon that just melts and spits out gold like a hot glue gun. That would be ridiculous, expensive, and so heavy you couldn't carry it.

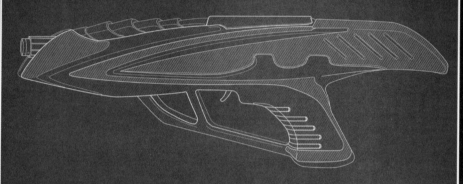

But what if . . . what if I could create something that could alter the chemicals in the air to a substance that actually mimicked gold.

That's too crazy to work, right? Right? Oh man, I've got to find more paper around here . . .

The Rogues eventually let Cisco and Dante go, but first they tortured Dante until Cisco gave up my secret identity. I was able to make a deal with Captain Cold, promising not to take him in as long as he refrained from lethal force. It was a deal with the devil, but at least it was a devil I knew.

Captain Cold and the Golden Glider. Mark and Clyde Mardon. Seems crime is often a family business here.

STR

ALIAS
James Jesse

POWERS/ABILITIES
Genius-level intellect; master strategist; capable inventor and engineer; darkly sick sense of humor

HOMEWORLD/DIMENSION
Earth-1

WEAKNESSES
Susceptible to conventional attacks when unprepared

NAME
TRICKSTER

ALIAS
Axel Walker

POWERS/ABILITIES
Access to the original Trickster's weaponry; several underground connections; warped dark sense of humor

HOMEWORLD/DIMENSION
Earth-1

WEAKNESSES
Susceptible to conventional attacks when unprepared; wants to impress his family at all costs

NAME
TRICKSTER II

STR •••

ALIAS
Zoey Clark

POWERS/ABILITIES
Often partner of the original Trickster with access to his weaponry

HOMEWORLD/DIMENSION
Earth-1

WEAKNESSES
Susceptible to conventional attacks when unprepared

NAME

PRANK

Twenty years ago, the original Trickster caused a panic in Central City during a murder spree that caught the nation's attention just by how strange it all was. Back then he had a partner in crime, an unknown woman called Prank.

CAUGHT AT LAST

By Mark Napier

The manic killer allegedly responsible for at least ten deaths in the Central City metro area was apprehended today after an anonymous tip alerted officers to his location. James Jesse, infamous for his gaudy spandex costume and his bizarre trick- and toy-themed crimes, was better known to the public by his alter ego, the Trickster.

"I couldn't be prouder of our boys in blue," said Mayor

CONTINUED ON FOLLOWING PAGE

Central City met the second Trickster when he littered brightly wrapped packages by parachute over the city. The packages were explosives, but luckily I was on hand to help keep the damage to a minimum.

The second Trickster, Axel Walker, was following in the original's footsteps, using his arsenal to eventually break James Jesse out of jail. As it turned out, Axel was the son of the first Trickster and Prank, proving that the rotten apple doesn't fall far from the tree.

REELECT

ANTHONY BELLOWS

VOTE!

At a fundraiser to reelect Mayor Anthony Bellows, the Tricksters drugged everyone's champagne, forcing the partygoers to transfer their assets to his bank account, which was written on the bottom of each glass.

When I showed up, the original Trickster strapped a bomb to me, but I was able to vibrate through a truck in order to safely detach the explosive. From there, it was a simple matter of injecting everyone with an antidote at super-speed before delivering both Tricksters back to jail.

ALIAS
Ray Palmer

POWERS/ABILITIES
Controls armored flight suit; genius-level intellect; suit now capable of shrinking in size along with its wearer; expert engineer and inventor; highly connected in the metahuman and business communities; member of the superhero team Legends, with access to their advanced technology

HOMEWORLD/DIMENSION
Earth-1

WEAKNESSES
Susceptible to conventional attacks when out of his armor

NAME

THE ATOM

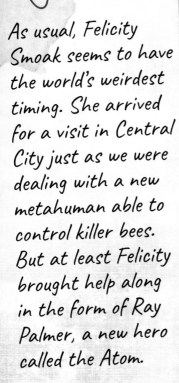

As usual, Felicity Smoak seems to have the world's weirdest timing. She arrived for a visit in Central City just as we were dealing with a new metahuman able to control killer bees. But at least Felicity brought help along in the form of Ray Palmer, a new hero called the Atom.

STR •••

ALIAS
Brie Larvan

POWERS/ABILITIES
Genius-level intellect; expert inventor and engineer; computer expert; former ties to Mercury Labs; designed and controls robotic bees loaded with poison and equipped with micro-cameras

HOMEWORLD/DIMENSION
Earth-1

WEAKNESSES
Susceptible to conventional attacks

STAR
LABORATORIES

FINGERPRINTS

RIGHT INDEX	RIGHT MIDDLE

NAME
BUG-EYED BANDIT

BILL CARLISLE - ROBOTS ENGINEER

EMAIL: B.CARLISLE@FOLSTONTECH.HU
PHONE: (816) 555-4912

I showed up too late to stop the Bug-Eyed Bandit from stinging her next victim, Bill Carlisle. But I was just in time to die myself, thanks to the same swarm of bees. Yep, I was dead. Fortunately, Cisco built a defibrillator into the suit for just such an occasion.

By examining one of the bees, we realized that they weren't insects at all but robots created by Brie Larvan. We weren't hunting for a metahuman; we were searching for a robotics genius who had been fired from Mercury Labs and wanted revenge.

With the help of Felicity and Ray, we stopped Brie before she could kill the head of Mercury Labs, Tina McGee.

Take Wing and Fly Solo

Lindsay Kang, an engineering professor at Hudson University, was stung to death in her car while on campus.

Hudson
University

In New Carthage

How do you stop a guy who can flawlessly shape-shift into anyone he touches? Worse, when he impersonates a friend of yours and kills two cops, how do you prove that friend is innocent?

That was the case with the particle accelerator metahuman known as Everyman. The man he framed? Eddie Thawne. We caught up to Everyman at the airport, and thanks to Caitlin's serum, we were able to prove the real Eddie Thawne innocent.

S.T.A.R.
LABORATORIES

SUBJECT: Everyman

The best way to stop our shape-shifter is to block his abilities. He can't elude the Flash if he can't blend in seamlessly with a crowd.

The question remains, is it possible to create a serum that could terminate the polymerization reaction? Essentially forcing the bonds to revert to their original form? Depriving his cells of their electrical charge would stop him from being able to control his power, at least for a time. And then our guy goes from Everyman to just man.

That's right. I can nickname, too.

STR •••

ALIAS
Hannibal Bates

POWERS/ABILITIES
Able to shape-shift into anyone he touches

HOMEWORLD/DIMENSION
Earth-1

WEAKNESSES
Powers can be negated by Caitlin Snow's serum

NAME
EVERYMAN

District Attorney Cecile Horton couldn't ignore the dashboard camera footage of Thawne shooting two fellow cops in cold blood. So while Eddie was incarcerated, Everyman was posing as everyone, from Eddie to me.

You know, it was almost ridiculous that Iris didn't know my secret and nearly everyone else in my life did. Here I was, keeping this huge secret from Iris, who has been my best friend since I was a boy. All in some misguided attempt to keep her safe. She was probably safer when she finally learned the truth.

Back when I was in a coma, Iris touched my hand and felt a shock. Not static electricity, but something . . . else. When the Flash touched her hand with the same effect, she put two and two together, and suddenly it all made sense.

That doesn't mean she wasn't mad when she finally confronted me at STAR Labs, though.

Not gonna lie. Seeing Iris's and Eddie's names on a return label was sort of like a punch in the face. Can't imagine how I'd feel if the label read "Iris and Eddie Thawne."

Iris West & Eddie Thawne
203-2320 Western Avenue
Central City, USA
74912

GIANT GORILLA IN THE SEWER

By Sergius Hannigan

CENTRAL CITY – Two Central City maintenance workers were reported missing after a routine inspection in the city's sewers near 5th Avenue and 10th Street, sources close to City Hall say. While the workers' names were omitted from official reports as of this writing, *The National Whisper* has learned that their abductor just might be the mysterious seven-foot gorilla that both the police and the mayor's office deny exists.

This has not been the first reported case of a hairy beast living in the city's complex sewer system. For months, rumors have circulated about a large shadowy beast, perhaps a former circus or zoo animal, highly evolved past the point of any known primate. However, no city official will go on record to acknowledge the gorilla's presence. An urban myth? A government cover-up? The first stage in an ape–human war? For now, no one is talking. Not even the gorilla.

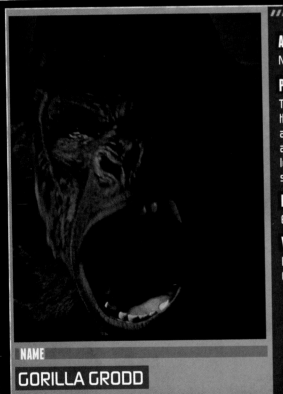

STR ●●●

ALIAS
No known alias

POWERS/ABILITIES
Telepathic and able to project thoughts into the minds of others; strength, durability, agility, and stamina of an extremely large and healthy gorilla; very intelligent; natural leader; enhanced intelligence and understands the English language

HOMEWORLD/DIMENSION
Earth-1

WEAKNESSES
His loyalty to Harrison Wells and Caitlin Snow

NAME

GORILLA GRODD

"Hey Flash, your life isn't messed up enough, what with dozens of metahumans appearing in your city, the love of your life in love with another man, and finding out time travel is an actual thing. Wanna fight a monkey?"

"Sure! Sounds great!" This was what my life was like when I met Gorilla Grodd. (And yes, I know gorillas aren't monkeys. I'm a scientist, remember?)

From: Harrison Wells <hwells@STARLabs.ccu>
To: General Wade Eiling <w.eiling@usarmy.ccu>
Subject: RE: Grodd

S.T.A.R.
CONFIDENTIAL
LABORATORIES

Eiling,

It is with little regret that I inform you our partnership has come to its close. While I had suspicions about your motives early on in our collaboration, I've recently reviewed a folder on Subject: Grodd left behind in Lab 2B by—I can only assume—one of your inferiors. While I believe this particular file was not intended for my eyes, I found it nevertheless enlightening.

Included in this horror show you so routinely label as "Experiment J" was photographic evidence of shocking abuse by your authority. The research conducted was in clear violation of the Animal Welfare Act. As a result, you or your subordinates will no longer be permitted on STAR Labs property from this day forth, and you will cease all communications with me or any of my employees.

In other words, find another lab to do your dirty work. I hope your wars are worth it, General.

Harrison Wells

When a mind-controlled General Eiling reappeared after a prolonged absence, we soon met Gorilla Grodd. Apparently, Wells and Eiling had partnered briefly while working on a secret project to expand soldiers' cognitive abilities, and Grodd was the unwitting test subject. Wells called off the partnership, but Grodd escaped STAR Labs after the particle accelerator explosion.

Meaning that thanks to Eiling's experiments and Wells's accelerator, Central City had a powerful psychic gorilla on its hands.

Cisco's tracking system for locating Grodd. It kept tabs on our locations while Team Flash coached me from STAR Labs.

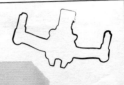

We were able to find a temporary home for Grodd in another dimension, a place run by apes called Gorilla City.

Solovar. I was tricked into defeating him once, allowing Grodd to step into a position of power. Grodd then immediately led an army of gorillas in an attack on Central City. But when we helped Solovar challenge Grodd again for superiority, Grodd lost, and Solovar commanded his apes back to Gorilla City.

Joe was the first one to be suspicious. Something about Harrison Wells just struck him as off. I guess there is something to be said about a cop's gut instinct, because the Harrison Wells who had set off the particle accelerator, who had mentored Cisco and Caitlin, who had been there for me when I came out of my coma . . . he wasn't Wells at all.

STR • • •

NAME
REVERSE-FLASH

ALIAS
Eobard Thawne • Dr. Harrison Wells

POWERS/ABILITIES
Genius-level intellect; possesses scientific knowledge far beyond his years; access to STAR Labs' highly advanced technology and other genius-level employees; can move at superhuman speeds; super-fast healing; able to create tornados or other cyclones by moving his limbs at super-speed; can vibrate through solid objects; able to run so fast he can go back or forward in time (usually with aid of tachyon enhancements)

HOMEWORLD/DIMENSION
Earth-1

WEAKNESSES
Standard human strength and durability makes him susceptible to a wide variety of attacks when unprepared; vulnerable to Time Wraiths like any speedster

• •

Eobard Thawne.
The real face of the
Reverse-Flash, and
a descendant of
Eddie Thawne.

The Reverse-Flash was faster than me. He was smarter than me. But it didn't matter. He killed my mother. I wasn't just going to let him walk—or run—away.

SUBJECT: AUDIOLOG 7048-2

AUDIOLOG: REVERSE-FLASH

I'm beginning to worry that Barry and the others are getting too close to the truth. I guess this was always destined to happen, but I'm surprised it's proceeding this quickly. Oh well, it only accelerates my timeline. And as you know, Gideon, I do like things fast.

In an effort to collect my thoughts, I'll once again reiterate how we got to this point:

As you know, I come from the future—most recently, the year 2024, but originally much further ahead than that. The Flash is my opposite, my reverse; the one man in the universe I absolutely and completely hate.

Once I found out his name, I knew how to finally defeat him. I sped back in time to kill his younger self, but he followed me. When the Flash ran his younger self out of his house, I killed his mother instead, thinking the tragedy would prevent Barry from ever becoming the Flash. But I was wrong. That was the very incident that made the Flash into who he is. Into who I despise. To make matters worse, I was trapped powerless in the past, forced to wait around until the Flash gained his powers and could help me return to my time.

However, I needed to speed things up. So I took over the role of Harrison Wells after killing both Wells and his wife. That way I could activate the particle accelerator years before it was intended to work, thereby helping the Flash gain super-speed as a young man. Things are finally coming together now. He's almost fast enough to get me where I need to go.

To finally get me home.

CLASSIFIED

An excerpt from the Reverse-Flash's audiolog. Trust me, it's not something you want to listen to from start to finish. Even listening at increased speed doesn't make it any less creepy.

Since the Reverse-Flash was hiding in plain sight, it only made sense that his headquarters was right under our noses, too. Called the Time Vault, Thawne stored his Reverse-Flash suit there and interfaced with Gideon, an artificially intelligent computer system, all from inside a secret chamber at STAR Labs.

The Centr

NEWS FEED | NATIONAL | WORLD | BUS

"Harrison Wells" was never paralyzed. It was all part of the Reverse-Flash's ruse, and a way to charge his powers using tachyon technology in his wheelchair.

FLAS
VANIS

BY IRIS WEST-ALLEN
THURSDAY, APRIL 25, 2024

After an extreme street battle with the Reverse-Flash, our city's very own Scarlet Speedster disappeared in an explosion of light. The cause of the fight is currently unknown. According to witnesses, The Flash, with help from Starling City's Green Arrow, The Atom, and Hawkgirl, began fighting the Reverse-Flash around midnight last night. The sky took on a deep crimson color as the ensuing battle created the most destruction this city has seen since The Flash first arrived in Central City.

Several trucks were caught in the fray, spilling their contents into the street. Power outages swept nearly twenty city blocks, between 16th street and Adams Avenue. Five of those blocks still remain without power. All of the buildings in the area were evacuated by the CCPD, with additional help from The Atom.

According to reports, as The Flash and Reverse-Flash battled with each other between

ul City Ci

MISSING
ES IN CRISIS

The smoke from the truck's engine made it difficult to see, but it appeared at one point they were having a very heated conversation before continuing the fight. Then, suddenly, The Flash sped after Reverse-Flash, and the two vanished, leaving The Atom, Green Arrow and Hawkgirl behind.

An eyewitness who watched the battle from her apartment building before being evacuated, said, "It was hard to see, but The Flash and Reverse-Flash were zipping up and down Monroe Avenue and then there was a whole bunch of lightning, and then nothing. It was weird."

Other witnesses described a similar phenomenon: a blinding light followed by darkness. Then the sky returned to black. And as the streets quieted, it took only a moment to realize The Flash and the Reverse-Flash were gone without a trace.

Central City Police Chief, Joe West, held a press conference in the wee hours of the morning stating, "We don't have very many details right now. What we do know is tonight Central City's greatest protector vanished in a flash. We can only hope he returns just as quickly." A sentiment shared by all who call this great city home.

The Reverse-Flash
initiated his endgame,
but I wasn't going to face
him alone. With the help
of Firestorm and Arrow,
we took him down and
successfully imprisoned
him in the Pipeline.

S.T.A.R.
LABORATORIES

Eobard Thawne needed my speed to create a stable wormhole to return to his future. Even after we caught him, he expected me to go along with his plan, suggesting I use the wormhole to go back in time and save my mother.

The bait was too good to resist. I took Eobard's deal, and helped him create his wormhole.

:WORMHOLE.STATUS
// → STABLE

I ran back to the past. I saw my mother. I saw the Reverse-Flash and my future self locked in battle. But then the future Flash saw me.

He raised his hand, and with that small gesture and the shake of his head, I realized that I wasn't meant to save my mother.

I had to stand by as Thawne killed her. I had to relive the worst day of my life. But since I was there, I could still do something.

I held my mother as she died. I gave her comfort, told her I would be okay. And then I ran back to my world.

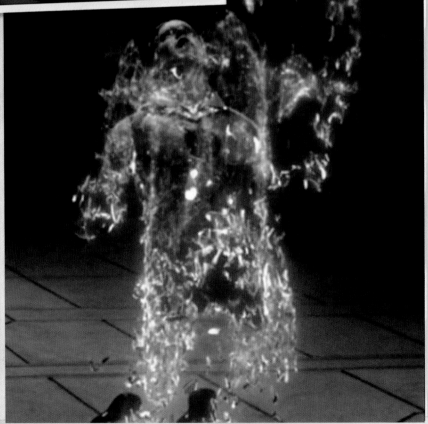

CENTRAL CITY POLICE
INCIDENT RE...
S.T.A.R.
CONFIDE...
LABORATO...

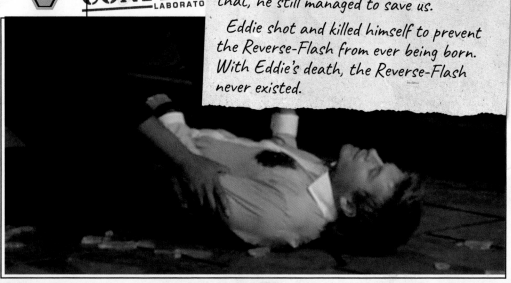

CENTRAL CITY POLICE DEPART...
CRIME SCENE REPORT

Before his death, Eobard Thawne had admitted to feeling some pride in the person I had become. He hated the Flash from his future, but he'd somehow become "fond" of me.

Yeah, I don't get it either. Guess that's why I'm not a criminal genius.

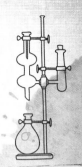

As a sort of farewell gift, Thawne had recorded a video confession as Wells, admitting to killing my mother. It was enough evidence for the police to reevaluate my dad's case.

The next thing I knew, Henry Allen was set free.

Dad's return home was short-lived at first. He needed some time to gather himself before he could return to life in Central City. Just like me, Dad needed to keep moving.

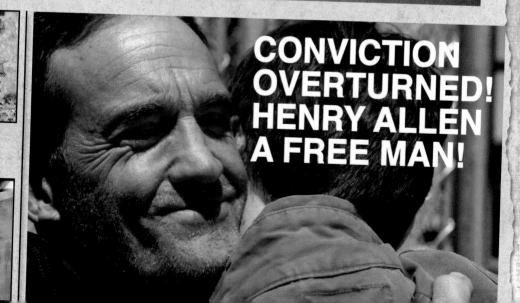

Central City

Picture News

CONVICTION OVERTURNED! HENRY ALLEN A FREE MAN!

Six months after the singularity, the city wanted to honor the Flash any way that it could. But two of my friends were dead and I was still here. It didn't seem fair.

I wasn't in the mood to celebrate.

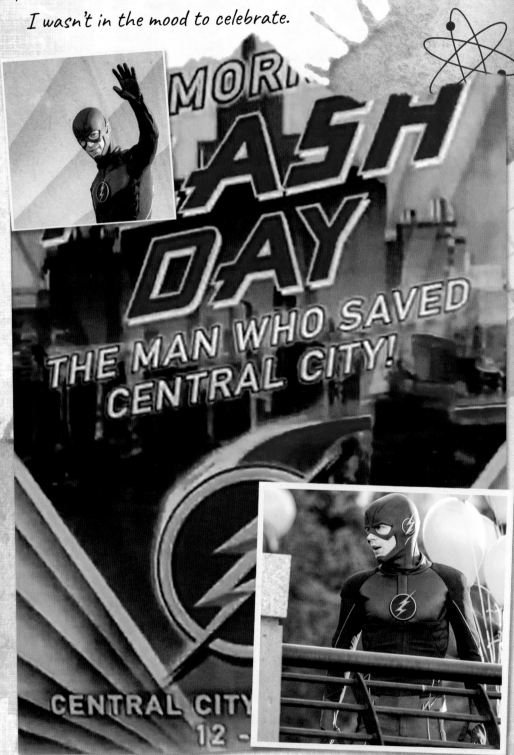

After everything happened, I couldn't slow down. I spent my nights reconstructing the city at super-speed. But after a talk with Iris, I realized the city needed to see me more than I didn't want to be seen.

So I showed up, and I let them cheer. And I let them give me the key to the city. And for the first time since the singularity, I let myself feel good again.

After the singularity, Team Flash temporarily split up. Too much had happened. Cisco began working with the Central City Police Department as a cientific advisor for Joe's new metahuman task force, even if Captain Singh wasn't crazy about Cisco's personal . . . let's call it flair?

Behold, the B.O.O.T.! A one-size-fits-all metahuman power nullifier. Now can somebody please get me a police badge? C'mon! I've earned it!
-Cisco

But after Flash Day, Iris realized that Central City didn't just need Flash. It needed Team Flash. That meant getting Cisco back from the CCPD and Caitlin back from her new job at Mercury Labs. Even Professor Stein was recruited.

The band had gotten back together, whether I wanted them to or not. Deep down, I totally wanted them to.

ITEM	FLASH SIGNAL		
SCHEMATIC	Cisco Ramon	NUMBER 499	

Introducing . . . the Flash Signal!
This is probably from a comic book somewhere, so I hope we don't get sued

100x more powerful than your standard searchlight

Bulletproof hand-ground glass for perfect clarity

While it's not really that practical when it comes to summoning the Flash—I mean, we've got the dude's phone number-it could come in handy to notify allies or even as bait to lure in the bad guys

Also, can I keep it at my house? Not to play with or anything . . .
For emergencies

No, we didn't let Cisco keep the Flash Signal at his apartment. The last thing I need is to be summoned at 3 a.m. for a run to Big Belly Burger.

THE NEW SUIT

So the costume may or may not be inspired by the suit we saw in the Reverse-Flash's future newspaper. Okay, it definitely is. But that's cool. We've got no reason to fear the future these days. Anyway, check this out:

New white logo really helps the lightning bolt pop

New heated function to unfreeze Barry in case of a supercold attack (I'm looking at you, Captain Cold)

Streamlined design to allow for even faster speeds (if that's even humanly possible, or should I say metahumanly possible)

Automatically updates status to PictureGram. We can disable that if you guys want. Yeah, I'm just gonna go ahead and disable that now

Future me knew what he was doing. The new brighter suit really is way more my speed.

Oh god. I'm starting to sound like Cisco. I really need to make some nonwork friends.

Just when you think you're the only Flash in town, a new guy shows up, claiming he's the Flash from an alternate dimension called Earth-2.

Jay Garrick came to STAR Labs after watching us for months. He claimed to be a speedster on his world but was stranded here when the singularity we created sucked him through a dimensional breach and left him without his powers.

STR ●●●

ALIAS
Jay Garrick ● ▬▬▬▬▬▬▬▬▬

POWERS/ABILITIES
(When not suffering power-loss): able to move at superhuman speeds; super-fast healing; able to create tornados or other cyclones by moving his limbs at super-speed; can vibrate through solid objects; genius-level intellect

HOMEWORLD/DIMENSION
Earth-2

WEAKNESSES
Standard human strength and durability makes him susceptible to a wide variety of attacks when unprepared; experienced loss of super-speed when traveling to Earth-1

NAME
THE FLASH

Jay warned us about Zoom, an evil speedster on his world who wanted nothing more than to steal my speed.

10:08 Looks like Cisco is working on updating the security at STAR Labs today. Caitlin's already been working on it for a good two hours. No sign of Barry. Late again?

11:15 Attempted B&E on Bates Street. Suspect found tied to a lamppost with bungee cords from the home's garage. No doubt Barry's handiwork.

11:17 Purse returned to woman on Jensen Avenue. A perp had stolen it not twenty seconds before. The woman reported not even knowing the purse was gone.

12:04 Barry having lunch outside Central City Police Department. Tried eating alone but is joined by Joe West. Doesn't seem to mind the company.

12:09 In the middle of their meal, a man in Joe's handcuffs appears in front of them with a garbage bag of money on his lap. Not sure what heist he was attempting, but both Joe and Barry find this amusing.

1:39 Back at STAR, Cisco is on the rooftop of the building. I think he's working on satellite feeds, but for the most part, he just seems to be dancing.

2:53 Iris West spotted at a C.C. Jitters temporary pop-up stand. She's talking on a cell phone. Sounds like she's taking a witness statement.

4:45 Stakeout at Barry's home. No movement in quite some time.

7:08 Checked out a rumored attack by Captain Cold in the Diamond District. Turned out to be a false alarm. Some vendor left his ice cream truck parked on the street. Over police blotter, I hear chatter of a bar fight broken up by a streak of lightning.

9:54 Barry's already started his reconstruction work for the evening. This time, it's at the Mercury Labs storage facility. Might as well head back. He'll be at this all night.

Yeah, I thought his notes were a little stalkery at first, too. But I guess the Flash from Earth-2 wanted to be sure he could trust us before introducing himself. Or at least that's what he said.

Once I started to let my guard down around Jay, he taught me plenty of tricks. One of them was the ability to charge up the Speed Force enough to throw an actual lightning bolt. I will never get tired of how cool that is.

For decades, scientists have posited the multiverse theory. It's the idea that other dimensions exist in the same space as our own, but they vibrate on a different frequency.

Having accidentally created an alternate timeline myself when fighting the Weather Wizard—sorry again about that—I already had a pretty good idea that other universes existed. But when we met the Flash of Earth-2, my hypothesis was confirmed.

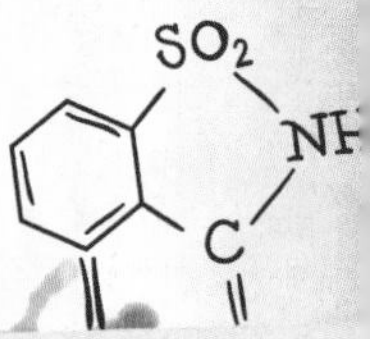

Multiverse Theory

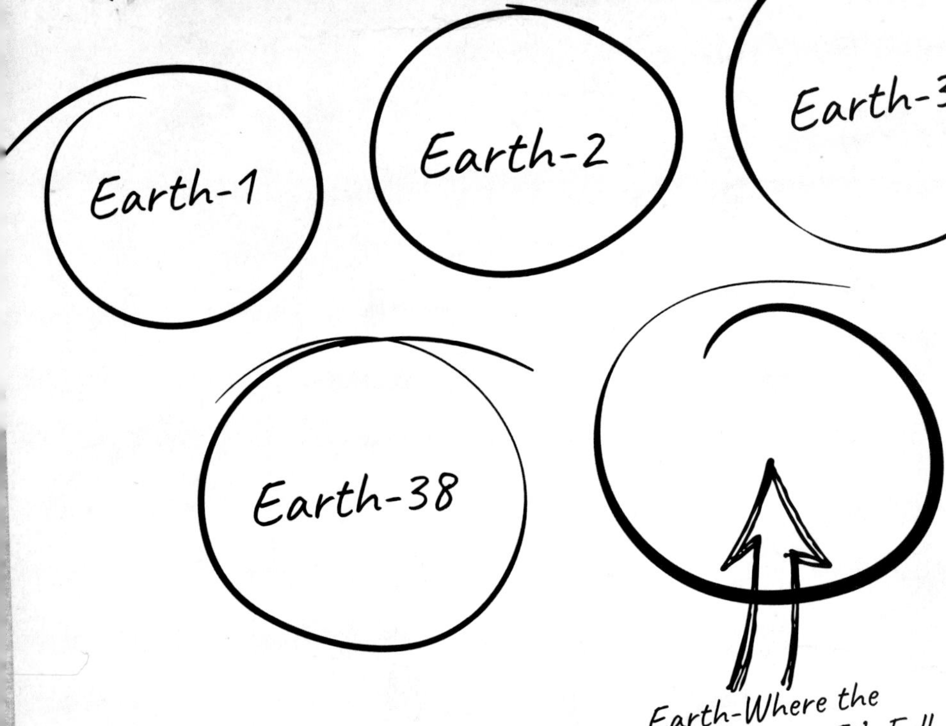

Earth-1

Earth-2

Earth-3

Earth-38

Earth-Where the Nazis Win or It's Full of Talking Animals or Something

We know there are about 52 worlds in total. We also know there are certain people who can breach those dimensions. We just don't know much about them yet . . .

While Joe couldn't quite wrap his head around the multiverse theory, he did get some new help with his metahuman task force in the form of Officer Patty Spivot.

Patty and I dated for a while, but when she suspected I was the Flash and I wouldn't admit it, she left town for a new life, starting over at Midway City University.

Zoom's main plan of attack involved forcing Earth-2 metahumans to travel through the dimensional breach into our world. If they wanted to get home, they had to kill me. **So that was fun . . .**

STR

ALIAS
Al Rothstein

POWERS/ABILITIES
Super-strength; endurance, stamina, and durability; able to grow in size; wears armored helmet; can absorb atomic power

HOMEWORLD/DIMENSION
Earth-2

WEAKNESSES
Powers can be overloaded by absorbing too much radiation

NAME
ATOM-SMASHER

Every party needs a crasher. Flash Day was crashed by Atom-Smasher, after Rothstein killed his Earth-1 doppelgänger. I was able to give the guy an overdose of radiation only with the help of the newly reunited Team Flash.

STR

ALIAS
Eddie Slick

POWERS/ABILITIES
Made entirely of sand-like cells; capable of rearranging and shape-shifting his form into various shapes and weapons

HOMEWORLD/DIMENSION
Earth-2

WEAKNESSES
Sand-like cells can be hardened and disabled by a lightning bolt

Sand Demon was another metahuman sent here by Zoom. When he kidnapped Patty Spivot, I teamed up with Jay Garrick to take him down via a lightning bolt.

NAME
SAND DEMON

STR

ALIAS
Dante Ramon

POWERS/ABILITIES
Wields powerful energy scythe

HOMEWORLD/DIMENSION
Earth-2

WEAKNESSES
Can be rendered powerless when disarmed

The Earth-2 doppelgänger of Dante Ramon blamed Cisco for the death of his world's Cisco Ramon. Yeah, I know. It gets confusing. Either way, Zoom killed Rupture when he didn't prove as capable as Zoom had expected.

NAME
RUPTURE

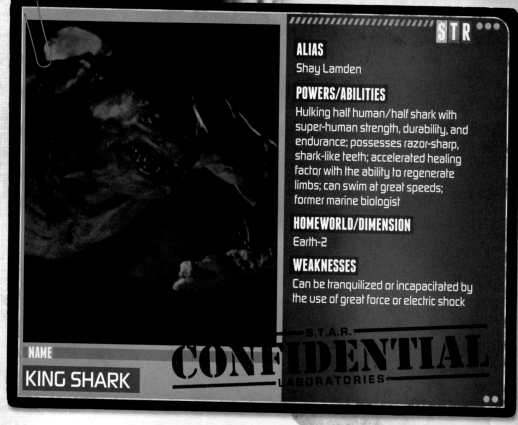

ALIAS
Shay Lamden

POWERS/ABILITIES
Hulking half human/half shark with super-human strength, durability, and endurance; possesses razor-sharp, shark-like teeth; accelerated healing factor with the ability to regenerate limbs; can swim at great speeds; former marine biologist

HOMEWORLD/DIMENSION
Earth-2

WEAKNESSES
Can be tranquilized or incapacitated by the use of great force or electric shock

S.T.A.R.

CONFIDENTIAL

LABORATORIES

NAME
KING SHARK

King Shark. He's a shark man who really wants to eat me. That's about all you need to know about this particular Zoom recruit from Earth-2.

King Shark is a major threat out of the ocean, but in his natural element, he's even deadlier. After he escaped ARGUS's confinement, I was only able to stop him by creating a vortex around him and electrifying the water. Even then I got too close to those jaws for comfort.

Director Michaels,

We've had a small breach in security. Or a rather large one, to be more accurate. The metahuman Lamden, Shay—commonly called King Shark—has escaped the Aquarium.

We're not sure how many of our staff he's . . . he's eaten at this time. I would await further instructions, but I'm leaving you this note to let you know I've decided to take a sick day for the rest of the afternoon. I've . . . got a cough. Or something.

I'll probably be back tomorrow, depending on the . . . cough.

Agent Perez

ALIAS
No known alias

POWERS/ABILITIES
Genius-level intellect; expert engineer and inventor; connections at both STAR Labs of Earth-1 and Earth-2; highly respected in the scientific community; father of Jesse Quick

HOMEWORLD/DIMENSION
Earth-2

WEAKNESSES
Susceptible to conventional attacks

NAME

DR. HARRISON "HARRY" WELLS

STAR LABORATORIES

FINGERPRINTS

RIGHT INDEX	RIGHT MIDDLE

An adversary of Jay Garrick's, Harry Wells showed up on Earth-1 to help us take down Zoom. It took a while, but we all finally came around to Harry despite his holier-than-thou attitude and his more than passing resemblance to the evil Dr. Wells we all knew.

Harry's daughter, Jesse. Wells used to call her his little "Jesse Quick." Zoom found Harry's true weakness when he kidnapped her.

SUBJECT: Dr. Wells

I normally don't like to judge a book by its cover. That's not me. But let's say you read a book, and it was just awful. Like the worst book ever. Then that book murdered a few of your friends and your best friend's mom, and all the while, that book pretended to be your mentor for its own sick amusement. If you saw that particular book again, it'd be okay to judge the heck out of it, right?

I mean seriously, this guy pops in out of nowhere, says he's not our evil murderous Dr. Wells, and then is such a condescending jerk about literally everything. And we're supposed to trust him?

Nah, there's something up with him. He's holding something back, and I'm worried that by the time we figure out what it is, it'll be too late.

Maybe we just go ahead and burn this particular book, you feel me?

—Cisco

I always laugh when other people change their relationship status to "it's complicated." Until you've met the Earth-2 doppelgänger of the girl you used to date, you really have no idea how complicated things can get.

STR

ALIAS
Linda Park

POWERS/ABILITIES
Can create light blasts from her hands; able to cause blinding effects; invisibility; expert computer hacker

HOMEWORLD/DIMENSION
Earth-2

WEAKNESSES
Can be confused by multiple targets in the form of speed mirages

NAME
DR. LIGHT

THE CENTRAL CITY CITIZEN

WHO IS YOUR META-MATCH? SPOTLIGHT ON THE LUMINOUS DR. LIGHT

Another of Zoom's recruits, Dr. Light wasn't the same breed of deadly criminal as the other Earth-2 villains. That all changed when she accidentally killed someone when trying to murder her own Earth-1 doppelgänger.

Dr. Light blinded me when we first met, but thanks to my accelerated healing abilities, I was able to face her again, running so fast that I created a speed mirage, effectively giving her too many targets to hit.

Every time I think I've seen all the crazy this world has to offer, the universe throws something else insane in my general direction. One of those blips on the crazy meter was Vandal Savage, a man who had been alive since the days of ancient Egypt and busied himself with murdering a pair of reincarnated soul mates throughout the centuries. I know, right?

STR •••

ALIAS

Hath-Set • Dr. Curtis Knox • Sasha Mahnovski

POWERS/ABILITIES

Seemingly immortal and can't be killed by conventional means, including illnesses and diseases; healing factor; expert martial artist in dozens if not hundreds of styles; weapons expert; expert marksman; tactical expert; naturally charismatic leader; thousands of connections in high-ranking societies due to his old age; genius-level intellect; commands vast network of lackey

HOMEWORLD/DIMENSION

Earth-1

WEAKNESSES

Meteorite radiation; ancient weapons originally wielded by Hawkman or Hawkgirl

NAME

VANDAL SAVAGE

It took the combined efforts of Team Arrow and Team Flash to take down Savage, but only after I sped through time again, effectively giving us a second chance to beat him. Even that wasn't the last we'd see of him. To really keep Savage down once and for all, it was going to take a whole different team of superheroes.

Speedy and Black Canary

Are we married to the name Speedy? I know she's Green Arrow's sidekick or sister or whatever, but Speedy sounds more like someone from the Flash family tree. How about Red Arrow? Or Arrowette?

—Cisco

And while we're talking Team Arrow, did Black Canary ever say anything about the sweet Canary Cry I designed for her?

—Cisco

A time traveler named Rip Hunter recruited a group of heroes to help him fight Vandal Savage and others like him. The team roster has changed over the years, but their goal has remained a constant: to protect the time stream.

And to sometimes do a little period-piece sightseeing or light theft/souvenir shopping. But who am I to judge? I've messed up the timeline plenty in my day.

Rip Hunter. Former Time Master, expert time traveler, and shepherd of their ship, the Waverider.

These two look familiar? I'm just happy to have Captain Cold and Heat Wave out of my city. They're Rip's problem now.

Now able to shrink in his Atom suit, Ray Palmer became a Legend. I never thought he and Felicity were a good fit, anyway . . .

Unable to survive without a partner, Professor Stein merged with Jefferson Jackson, another victim of the particle accelerator explosion. The two became the new Firestorm.

Kendra Saunders and Carter Hall, Hawkgirl and Hawkman, respectively. They've been reincarnated over the centuries, always destined to die at Vandal Savage's hand. They aimed to change that with the Legends' help.

The original Canary, White Canary was killed and then brought back to life. An assassin without a home, she eventually became the captain of the Waverider.

A later recruit, Steel can change his body to metal—a helpful trait when fighting, let's say, pirates or medieval knights.

Zari Tomaz. To be honest, I don't know much about her yet, but I hear she's an expert hacker from the future with a mystical "air totem." Sounds about par for the course for these guys.

The grandmother of the current Vixen (don't ask—it's a long story), with animal powers and a history of fighting as part of the world's first superhero team, the Justice Society of America.

His name is Russell Glosson. He is the slowest man alive.

Cisco had been working on a case about a metahuman thief he called the Turtle for a while. Originally, Cisco thought the Turtle could move at superhuman speed. But he actually had the ability to slow down everything around him. With the threat of Zoom looming as the constant elephant in the room at STAR, Cisco figured that the Turtle might just have the answers we were looking for.

STR •••

ALIAS
Russell Glosson

POWERS/ABILITIES
Able to slow those around him, yet cannot slow time itself

HOMEWORLD/DIMENSION
Earth-1

WEAKNESSES
His powerful slow barrier can be pierced with the use of super-speed

NAME
THE TURTLE

REC

Cisco tracked the Turtle down to the Naydel Library, where the guy lived among all his stolen trophies. I powered through his "slowness" barrier and knocked him out, taking him to the Pipeline.

What I didn't know at the time was that Dr. Wells had made a deal with Zoom to save his daughter Jesse's life. Zoom tasked Wells with "fattening" me up by increasing my speed powers so that Zoom would have more to steal from me.

To that end, Wells killed the Turtle to take a sample of his brain matter in order to develop a way to steal my speed.

Dropped in a vat of boiling tar right before the particle accelerator exploded, Joey Monteleone was transformed into Tar Pit. It was no surprise that Joey wanted revenge against the men who "killed" him.

STR

ALIAS
Joseph Monteleone

POWERS/ABILITIES
Able to drown his victims in tar produced from his body, effectively fossilizing them; body made up entirely of liquid tar; can turn from human form to liquid tar at will; able to generate heat and throw fireballs; can turn into a large hulking monster made of molten tar

HOMEWORLD/DIMENSION
Earth-1

WEAKNESSES
Body hardens in cold temperatures

NAME
TAR PIT

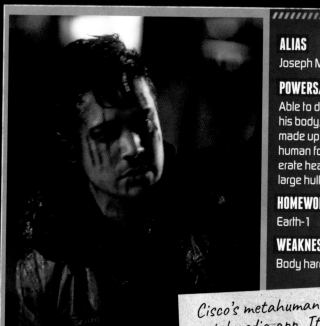

Cisco's metahuman social media app. It alerts his phone to any online discussions about metahuman sightings. It's actually way more helpful than I thought it'd be.

NEWS FEED >
Meta weirdo at 6ᵗʰ and...
Tar maniac on the street!
Meta-human spotted!
Black eyed freak...
Is this guy covered in...

While he could form himself into a molten tar monster, Tar Pit was no match for a few well-placed nitrous grenades. They caused him to revert to human form, where he then proved susceptible to a well-placed Joe West punch.

Barry and Cisco's Excellent Adventure to Earth-2!

POLICE

Look at our girl Iris, all copped-up like her dad.

Not only that, but Iris and not-fast-at-all Barry are married in this dimension. Ouch.

My doppelgänger, Reverb, is such a buzzkill, man. I mean, he works for Zoom, he's more powerful than me, and he talks in a ridiculous voice. Just when I was starting to like Earth-2.

Deadshot is a cop here! Assassin-for-hire-I-fight-the-Green-Arrow Deadshot. And he's the worst shot on the force. The irony is strong in this one.

Joe is my favorite doppelgänger of all time. He's a lounge singer at Jitterbugs, the C.C. Jitters of Earth-2. I am so going to frame this picture.

Ronnie's still alive on Earth-2, but here he's the villain Deathstorm, which has to be the name of a German metal band.

And mark my words, if Caitlin ever turns into a stone-cold villain like Killer Frost, I'm gonna retire from this whole super-hero lifestyle. You can quote me on that.

After a little sightseeing, Barry was taken captive by Zoom. Harry Wells and I teamed with Earth-2 Iris and Barry to track down Zoom's super creepy hideout.

With help from a thoroughly ticked off Killer Frost, we got our Barry and Harry's daughter out of that mess, and made it back to Earth-1.

Every super creepy hide-out needs a super creepy dude in an iron mask. I don't know what this guy's deal is, and I'm not sure I want to know.

Barry promised to go back and save him, though. And that, ladies and gentlemen, is why I'll never be as good as the Flash.

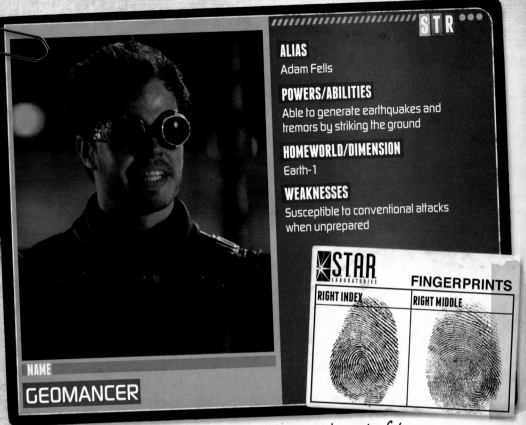

ALIAS
Adam Fells

POWERS/ABILITIES
Able to generate earthquakes and
tremors by striking the ground

HOMEWORLD/DIMENSION
Earth-1

WEAKNESSES
Susceptible to conventional attacks
when unprepared

STAR LABORATORIES

FINGERPRINTS

RIGHT INDEX	RIGHT MIDDLE

NAME

GEOMANCER

Geomancer started trouble when I was, uh, out of town.
Fortunately, Joe West and Jay Garrick were on hand to stop
him before he shook the city to rubble.

Thanks to Caitlin's
artificial speedster serum,
Velocity-9, Jay was able
to power up and face
Geomancer when he began
to up his game and raze
buildings. Geomancer took
his grudge to STAR Labs
next, but Caitlin was more
than able to hold her
own, eventually shooting
Geomancer with Cisco's
metahuman nullifying
B.O.O.T.

CENTRAL CITY POLICE DEPARTMENT

CENTRAL CITY POLICE

EVIDENCE:_____

When a super-fast thief started robbing people in my city, I took it personally. There's only so much speedster competition a guy can take. Turns out, it wasn't a metahuman at all, but a scientist hopped up on Caitlin's Velocity-9 formula.

STR ●●●

ALIAS
Eliza Harmon

POWERS/ABILITIES
Uses Velocity-9 for artificial super-speed to mimic the abilities of the Flash; access to Mercury Labs' extensive technology; genius-level intellect

HOMEWORLD/DIMENSION
Earth-1

WEAKNESSES
Addicted to Velocity-9

NAME
TRAJECTORY

If I was angry at being outrun when I first met Trajectory, my anger started to fade once I got to know who she was. She was a junkie, addicted to the formula that would eventually kill her. In the end, she ran herself to death. Not the way I would have chosen to win that particular race.

Ever since I fought the Weather Wizard and created a divergent timeline, Cisco has been able to tap into metahuman powers that let him "vibe" into other dimensions. His powers are growing every day, and he keeps learning new ways to use them. But don't believe him if he tells you that he made up the name Vibe. That one was all me.

STR

ALIAS
Francisco "Cisco" Ramon

POWERS/ABILITIES
Genius-level intellect; inventor and mechanical expert; brilliant computer programmer and engineer; access to highly advantaged technology at STAR Labs; well-connected among the metahuman and scientific communities; can see into other dimensions via episodes called "vibes"; able to fire vibrational blasts; able to open portals into other dimensions

HOMEWORLD/DIMENSION
Earth-1

WEAKNESSES
Susceptible to conventional attacks when unprepared

NAME

VIBE

The perfect design!

Complete with the recalibrated goggles from Dr. Wells that let me open up portals to other dimensions.

Definitely getting a good vibe from this one.

That's some nice wordplay right there. Barry should pay more attention to my writing skillz. He might learn a thing or three.

Seriously. Cisco is the reason I make so many bad puns. If this isn't proof, I don't know what is.

With no idea how to defeat Zoom, I ran back to the past to impersonate myself. I figured the only way I could learn how to increase my speed was from the guy who taught me most everything I know about life as a speedster, Eobard Thawne, the Reverse-Flash.

LABORATORIES

Thawne was still impersonating Wells at the time, but it didn't take him long to see through my ruse. He agreed to help me anyway, and the result was the Tachyon Enhancer. With it I can run four times faster than before.

When I returned to the present, a Time Wraith followed me. Time Wraiths are ghostlike beings that hate speedsters and want to eliminate them when they mess with the timeline. When I returned to the present, the Pied Piper stopped the Wraith. Apparently, my messing with time turned the Piper into a good guy?

So it was a win/win . . . right?

CENTRAL CITY POLICE DEPARTMENT
EVIDENCE:

Zoom wanted my newly enhanced speed. And he made
sure I had no choice but to give it to him.

Joe had just been reunited with a
son he never knew he had, Wally
West. So when Zoom kidnapped
Wally, dragging the innocent
kid into our world, my back was
up against the wall. Zoom took
my powers, and I became Barry
Allen, the most average guy alive.

Zoom ran back to Earth-2,
kidnapping Caitlin in the process.
Before I could even adjust to being
powerless again, I was forced
to face a rapidly aging particle
accelerator metahuman named
Griffin Grey, who aged himself to
death during our fight.

I decided to let Wells reenact
the particle accelerator
incident to regain my powers.
Iris chose the moment before
the explosion to finally tell me
how she feels. Neither of us
has that timing thing down.

Wells reactivated the
accelerator and focused the
dark-matter explosion solely
on me. But it didn't work as
planned. I simply disintegrated
before their eyes.

Dark-matter feedback shot
through the hallway and
struck Jesse and Wally.
Luckily, they both survived
the incident.

Watching Trajectory spark blue lightning, I realized that Velocity-9 had a side effect, one visible in Zoom. It didn't take long to figure out that Zoom and "Jay Garrick" were one and the same, a theory solidified thanks to Cisco's vibes.

S T R

ALIAS
Hunter Zolomon • Jay Garrick (fake identity)

POWERS/ABILITIES
Genius-level strategist; can move at superhuman speeds; super-fast healing; able to create tornados or other cyclones by moving his limbs at super-speed; can vibrate through solid objects; access to a variety of Earth-2 metahumans, whom he blackmails into his service

HOMEWORLD/DIMENSION
Earth-2

WEAKNESSES
Standard human strength and durability makes him susceptible to a wide variety of attacks when unprepared; vulnerable to Time Wraiths like any speedster

NAME
ZOOM

Zoom had been keeping the real Jay Garrick in a cell at his Earth-2 headquarters, forcing him to wear an iron mask. Surprisingly, the real Jay is from Earth-3 and is actually a doppelgänger for my dad, Henry Allen.

S.T.A.R. LABORATORIES

SUBJECT: Zoom

ANALYSIS: Taking everything we know about Zoom's past into consideration, I was able to construct a rudimentary timeline. It's not much, but it's something. Hunter Zolomon lived with his mother while his father was at war.

When his father returned, he forced Hunter to watch as he murdered Hunter's mother. Hunter was only eleven.

Hunter grew up in the Central City Orphanage after his father was sent to prison.

He became a serial killer, convicted of 23 counts of murder.

After his trial, Hunter was sentenced to the St. Perez Mental Asylum for the Criminally Insane.

He was given daily electroshock therapy, and was receiving such "treatment" when the Earth-2 particle accelerator exploded, granting him super-speed.

He escaped, and Zoom was born.

CONFIDENTIAL
TOP SECRET

My friends thought I was dead, but I was really trapped in the Speed Force. When I finally came to terms with my mom's death and found my way back to Earth, I was ready to face Zoom.

Zoom was on a rampage on our Earth, taking over Central City in a show of brute force. He swarmed the streets with his Earth-2 metas, causing the press to refer to the chaos as a "Metapocalypse." Thanks to some STAR Labs ingenuity, we found a particular frequency to broadcast that rendered all Earth-2 metahumans unconscious. Zoom escaped, though.

Black Canary's Earth-2 doppelgänger, Black Siren. She razed Mercury Labs. Even still, I was able to get Dr. McGee out in time.

In a desperate attempt to try to turn me into someone like him, Zoom killed my dad. Just like the Reverse-Flash before him, he took the life of my parent.

Zoom wanted to race me, but it was all a ploy to charge the Magnetar invention stolen from Mercury Labs. He wanted to destroy every Earth but Earth-1.

I took Zoom up on his challenge, but when we were running, I ran back in time and created a time remnant of myself, a me from another point in time. My time duplicate died stopping the Magnetar, but it was enough to attract the attention of the Time Wraith that claimed Zoom for its own.

We beat Zoom, but to me, it felt like I just lost.

CENTRAL CITY
POLICE

CENTRAL CITY POLICE DEPARTMENT
EVIDENCE:_____

STR ⦁⦁⦁

ALIAS
Jay Garrick

POWERS/ABILITIES
Can move at superhuman speeds; super-fast healing; able to create tornados or other cyclones by moving his limbs at super-speed; can vibrate through solid objects; able to run so fast he can go back or forward in time

HOMEWORLD/DIMENSION
Earth-3

WEAKNESSES
Standard human strength and durability makes him susceptible to a wide variety of attacks when unprepared; vulnerable to Time Wraiths like any speedster

NAME
FLASH

When I tried to run back in time to fix everything again, Jay stopped me. He made me realize that if I kept trying to change things, I'd just make matters worse. I was stuck with the reality I'd made.

I thought I had put my mother's death behind me. But after seeing my dad die, reliving that specific moment again, it was the last straw. I was broken. So I did what I do when things get rough. I ran.

I ran back in time, and saved my mother's life. And everything changed in a flash.

In a new reality we'd later call Flashpoint, Wally West was the hero, not me. He was a Kid Flash fighting villains such as a speedster named Rival. I had my powers, but I was free of it all. Mom and Dad were alive, I was just starting to date Iris, and life had possibilities away from fighting crime. But when Wally was injured, I knew I had to go back and undo what I'd done.

So once again I ran back in time. I changed the world. But it didn't quite go back together the way I'd left it.

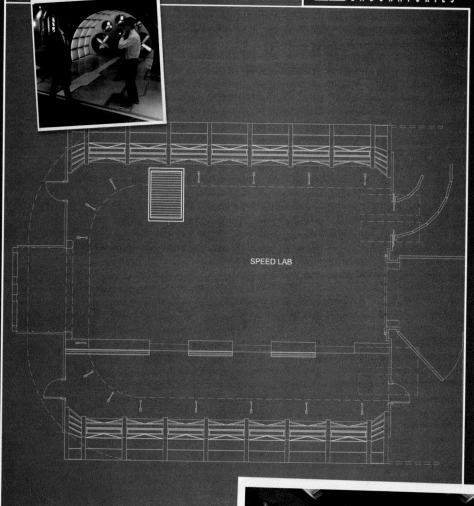

SPEED LAB

It was the little things that were different. STAR Labs had a sophisticated Speed Lab now, Joe and Iris were fighting, and I shared a lab at the CCPD with a metahuman CSI Specialist named Julian Albert.

But it got worse. Cisco's brother was dead. John Diggle had a son now instead of a daughter. And Caitlin . . . I can never make up for what I did to her.

In the wake of Flashpoint, Caitlin had a multiple personality disorder. Killer Frost was her dark side, always fighting to get out.

STR •••

ALIAS
Dr. Caitlin Snow

POWERS/ABILITIES
Able to generate extreme cold; can freeze victims or shoot ice from her body; accelerated healing factor while in Killer Frost form; genius-level intellect; expert medical knowledge

HOMEWORLD/DIMENSION
Earth-1

WEAKNESSES
Split personality between Snow and Frost personas creates constant inner turmoil and friction; Caitlin's personality slowly influencing Frost and becoming dominant

NAME
KILLER FROST

Cisco and Julian Albert designed a special necklace to inhibit Caitlin's Killer Frost side. It worked well for a time, but now Caitlin seems to have an agreement with her Frost persona, each giving the other the space she needs.

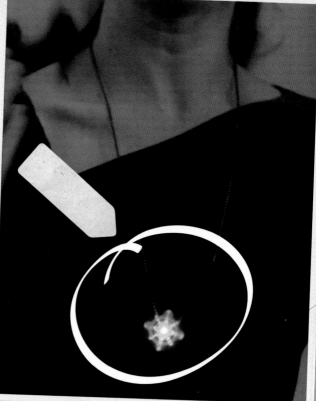

Today was a good day. Work was work, and not too eventful. Cisco and I have been developing a new theoretical breach detection system to alert us if we have interdimensional visitors to our Earth. But it's still a ways off from implementation. So kind of a slow day, which is fine with me. I'll take a break from the chaos whenever I can get one.

I think I'll call it an early night tonight and head to bed, after I read a chapter or two in my new Sapphire Stagg novel. Watch, I'll get myself into trouble and stay up reading for half the night!

—Caitlin

Oh my god, is Caitlin booooring. Ugh. She fell asleep at 8:30 with a pint of ice cream by her side. She'd only taken two bites from it. Watching our figure, I guess.

Anyway, I made sure her ice cream was good and frozen again before I headed out on the town. You owe me one, Caitlin.

So the night was pretty uneventful. I beat down some guy who had the audacity to try to take my purse. Okay, I wasn't carrying a purse. But in my defense, he did look at me funny. That's got to be a crime somewhere.

Tore my new jacket in the process, so by three in the morning I headed home. Finished off Caitlin's rocky road when I got back to the apartment. Consider that favor paid, Caitlin. Ugh. Brain freeze. Calling it a night.

—Killer Frost

They called him Alchemy. Well, everybody except for Cisco. He called our new metahuman creator _Doctor_ Alchemy.

STR

ALIAS
Julian Albert

POWERS/ABILITIES
Uses powerful mystic Philosopher's Stone to unlock Flashpoint reality powers in specific individuals; can fire energy blasts and mystic energy from the Stone

HOMEWORLD/DIMENSION
Earth-1

WEAKNESSES
Julian side of his personality does not want to continue Alchemy's criminal campaign

NAME
DR. ALCHEMY

Maybe it's only-child syndrome, or maybe it's the fact that Julian is only happy if he's talking down to me, but I never liked sharing my space with the guy. Especially when I found out the resident metahuman CSI Specialist was also a supervillain.

S.T.A.R. LABORATORIES

SUBJECT: *Philosopher's Stone*

EXPERIMENT #: *12689*

ANALYSIS: *Dr. Alchemy used the Philosopher's Stone to unlock the metahuman powers in people who had abilities during the Flashpoint reality.*

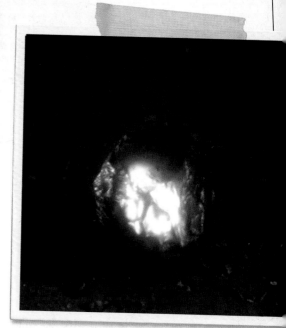

Alchemy wasn't the real threat. We later discovered that he was just working in the service of a darker master. Someone called Savitar (more on him later).

We were even able to later coax Julian onto Team Flash, ending Alchemy's career in the process.

Unlocking metahumans from the Flashpoint reality,
Dr. Alchemy did his best to make me run the proverbial
gauntlet. But hey, that's what I was born to do.

ALIAS
No known alias

POWERS/ABILITIES
Able to rapidly decompose his targets by making physical contact with them; bullets deteriorate on contact with his body

HOMEWORLD/DIMENSION
Earth-1

WEAKNESSES
Powers can be negated by a speedster vibrating through him, mingling his or her blood with Yorkin's

We met Clive Yorkin when he started killing people who were cops in the Flashpoint universe. Although we couldn't touch him, Yorkin could be stopped by vibrating through his form.

NAME
CLIVE YORKIN

ALIAS
Frankie Kane

POWERS/ABILITIES
Able to attract or repel metal objects by manipulating magnetics

HOMEWORLD/DIMENSION
Earth-1

WEAKNESSES
Suffers from split personality disorder; her Frankie persona can be reasoned with

When her powers unlocked and she nearly killed her foster father, Frankie Kane's Magenta persona took over. It took more than one speedster to stop the chaos she caused.

NAME
MAGENTA

ALIAS
No known alias

POWERS/ABILITIES
Vibrating at such a high frequency that he creates the illusion that he's a living shadow; able to hide in existing shadows; slows down molecules to take form and harden at will

HOMEWORLD/DIMENSION
Earth-1

WEAKNESSES
Bright light can cause him pain and force him to revert to human form

NAME

SHADE

Things came to a head with the metahuman killer Shade at the Central City Film Society's Movie in the Park night. We were able to force him back to his human form by putting the spotlight on him instead of the movie . . . literally.

ALIAS
Edward Clariss

POWERS/ABILITIES
Can move at superhuman speeds; super-fast healing; able to create tornados or other cyclones by moving his limbs at super-speed; can vibrate through solid objects

HOMEWORLD/DIMENSION
Earth-1

WEAKNESSES
Standard human strength and durability makes him susceptible to a wide variety of attacks when unprepared; vulnerable to Time Wraiths like any speedster

NAME

RIVAL

Kid Flash's archenemy from the Flashpoint timeline, Rival regained his speed powers and would have killed me if not for Vibe's last-second rescue/sweet team up.

ALIAS
Jesse Wells

POWERS/ABILITIES
Can move at superhuman speeds; super-fast healing; able to create tornados or other cyclones by moving her limbs at super-speed; can vibrate through solid objects

HOMEWORLD/DIMENSION
Earth-2

WEAKNESSES
Standard human strength and durability makes her susceptible to a wide variety of attacks when unprepared; vulnerable to Time Wraiths like any speedster

NAME

JESSE QUICK

Harry Wells and Jesse spent some time back on Earth-2 after the mess with Zoom was finally over. But when Jesse's super-speed powers were triggered, she and her dad came back to our world to better train her as a speedster.

Harry Wells was reluctant to let his daughter put on a suit and fight crime, but in the end, he realized he had no real choice. Jesse is her own person.

Man, I wish every costume design was this easy. Take Trajectory's old suit, throw on a Flash logo, and bam, instant hero.

—Cisco

Meanwhile, Iris and I finally started dating. I mean, it only took like what, fifteen years? Totally worth the wait.

Sam Scudder and his girlfriend Rosalind Dillon were hiding out at Broome Industries a few years ago when the particle accelerator first exploded. One wave of dark matter later, and they became the Bonnie and Clyde of Central City, the Mirror Master and the Top.

STR

ALIAS
Sam Scudder

POWERS/ABILITIES
Can travel through mirrors or reflective surfaces, and able to force others through these portals as well; can trap people in this "mirror dimension"; often partners with the Top; many underworld connections

HOMEWORLD/DIMENSION
Earth-1

WEAKNESSES
Anger can be used against him; Droste Effect—creating an infinite series of mirrors—can stop him from entering the mirror dimension; can be contained by using anti-reflective material

NAME
MIRROR MASTER

Mirror Master was trapped in a weird mirror dimension for three years before he broke out and teamed with the Top. But to him, it seemed like no time had passed.

I was able to set up a series of mirrors and create the Droste Effect to confuse the Mirror Master and beat him. Jesse Quick took out the Top by fighting off her vertigo effects.

Of course, that didn't stop the two of them from coming back time and time again, like true Central City Rogues.

STR •••

ALIAS
Rosalind Dillon

POWERS/ABILITIES
Able to induce crippling vertigo in her targets; often partners with Mirror Master; many underworld connections

HOMEWORLD/DIMENSION
Earth-1

WEAKNESSES
Susceptible to conventional attacks if vertigo symptoms are ignored or fought off

NAME
THE TOP

Mirror Master quickly freed the Top from Iron Heights using one of his reflective wormholes. Originally obsessed with getting revenge on Captain Cold, the pair soon learned of Cold's absence and began their own crime spree.

When Harry Wells opted to head back to Earth-2, he helped Cisco and Caitlin search the multiverse for a replacement. The result? H. R. Wells, a guy who seemed like the perfect Wells for our team. At least at first.

STR

ALIAS
No known alias

POWERS/ABILITIES
Charismatic; highly connected at STAR Labs; expert con man, if partially by accident; crossword puzzle expert; gifted idea man

HOMEWORLD/DIMENSION
Earth-19

WEAKNESSES
Susceptible to conventional attacks

NAME
H.R. WELLS

H. R. wasn't quite the person he advertised himself to be. While he certainly had a better sense of humor than our Wells, he was not a genius. He'd built his reputation off the work of others, and was only on Earth-1 to gain material for a new book he was writing.

One of H. R.'s first real contributions to STAR Labs was the creation of the STAR Labs Museum, a way for the team to bring in some revenue to help cover the insane costs of Team Flash.

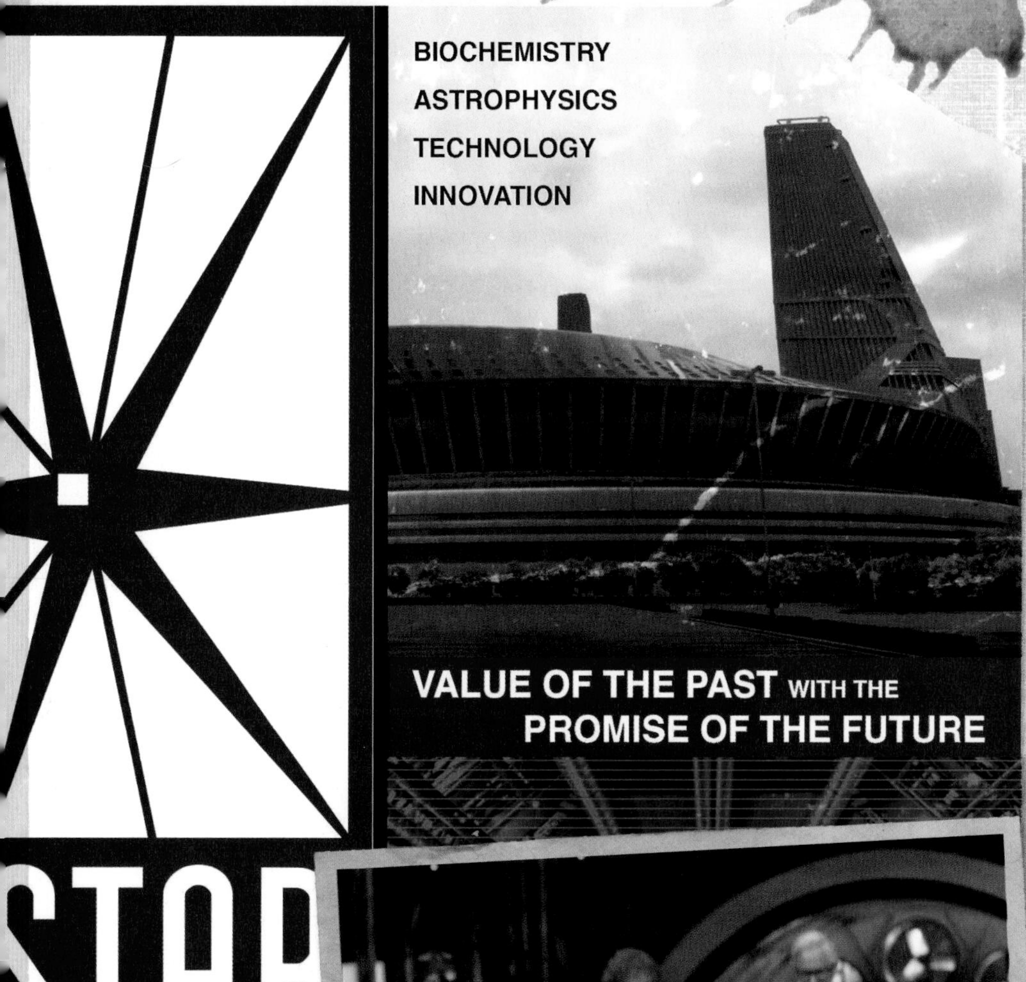

BIOCHEMISTRY
ASTROPHYSICS
TECHNOLOGY
INNOVATION

VALUE OF THE PAST WITH THE
PROMISE OF THE FUTURE

S.T.A.R
ABORATORIE
MUSEUM

Later, Harry consulted an entire Council of Wells from different Earths. Some of the brightest—if not altogether the strangest—minds the universe has ever known.

STR

ALIAS
Kara Zor-El • Kara Danvers

POWERS/ABILITIES
Super-strength, endurance, speed, agility, and durability; heat, microscopic, x-ray, and telescopic vision; accelerated healing; freeze breath; flight

HOMEWORLD/DIMENSION
Earth-38

WEAKNESSES
Kryptonite; red sun radiation; magic manipulation

NAME

SUPERGIRL

The first time I met Kara—or as Earth-38 calls her, Supergirl—I had accidentally run to her dimension, and needed a bit of help getting back.

We fought two of her villains, one called Livewire, and the other called Silver Banshee. It was so much fun, it was a shame that our next hangout was monopolized by evil invading aliens.

But hey, these things happen.

The Dominators, an alien race with eyes on conquering Earth ever since the 1950s, decided to wage a full-on invasion of our world. It took the combined efforts of Team Flash, Team Arrow, the Legends, and Supergirl to eventually defeat them. And no, _that's_ not as much fun as it sounds.

INVASION!
The Dominators Attack An Unsuspecting World
By Linda Park

I once got a chance to race the Girl of Steel. How awesome is that?

Oh, did I mention that we were also once trapped in a dreamworld thanks to an all-powerful villain called the Music Meister?

We had to literally fight our way through an old-timey musical to get back to the land of the living.

Superheroes live weird lives, man.

All his life, Wally West wanted to go fast. From wanting to be an astronaut as a kid, to participating in illegal drag racing, Wally needed speed in his life. But even though he was caught in the second particle accelerator explosion alongside Jesse Quick, he still didn't gain a speedster's powers.

STR

ALIAS
Wally West

POWERS/ABILITIES
Can move at superhuman speeds; super-fast healing; able to create tornados or other cyclones by moving his limbs at super-speed; can vibrate through solid objects

HOMEWORLD/DIMENSION
Earth-1

WEAKNESSES
Standard human strength and durability makes him susceptible to a wide variety of attacks when unprepared; vulnerable to Time Wraiths like any speedster

NAME
KID FLASH

CENTRAL CITY POLICE DEPARTMENT
SECURITY FOOTAGE

REC

Wally used to participate in illegal drag racing until Iris intervened and nearly died because of it.

When Wally touched Dr. Alchemy's Philosopher's Stone, he became encased in a weird, husk-like cocoon. Joe couldn't take seeing his boy like that, and broke Wally free.

It didn't matter that Wally arrived at his powers in the strangest way possible; to him, it just mattered that when he emerged from his cocoon, he was finally a speedster. As soon as he could, he adopted the identity of Kid Flash.

Wally and Jesse Quick dated for a little bit. When Jesse ended things via a break-up cube (some weird Earth-2 tradition), Wally took it kinda hard.

Later, Wally opted for some time alone to collect his thoughts. When Rip Hunter came calling, Wally ended up becoming a time traveling hero and carving his own way in the world as a Legend.

When he came to work at our STAR Labs, H. R. failed to mention that it was against the rules of his world, Earth-19, to hop dimensions. It was the job of "Collectors" to capture lawbreakers like him. One Collector in particular was assigned to his case, a woman called Gypsy.

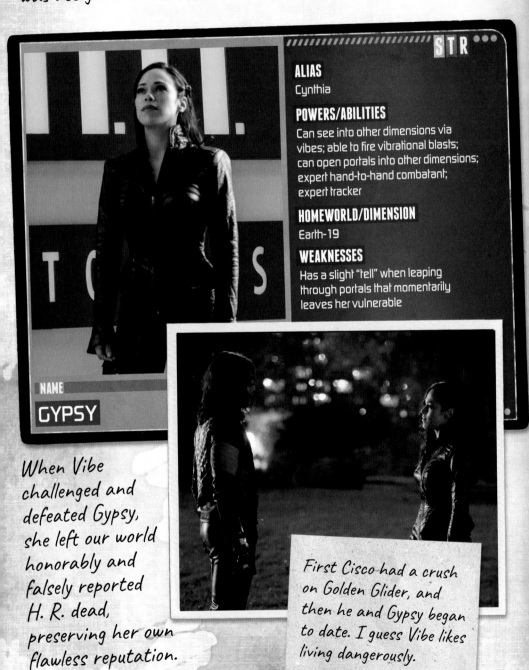

STR

ALIAS
Cynthia

POWERS/ABILITIES
Can see into other dimensions via vibes; able to fire vibrational blasts; can open portals into other dimensions; expert hand-to-hand combatant; expert tracker

HOMEWORLD/DIMENSION
Earth-19

WEAKNESSES
Has a slight "tell" when leaping through portals that momentarily leaves her vulnerable

NAME
GYPSY

When Vibe challenged and defeated Gypsy, she left our world honorably and falsely reported H. R. dead, preserving her own flawless reputation.

First Cisco had a crush on Golden Glider, and then he and Gypsy began to date. I guess Vibe likes living dangerously.

STR

ALIAS
Josh

POWERS/ABILITIES
Can see into other dimensions via vibes; able to fire vibrational blasts; can open portals into other dimensions; expert hand-to-hand combatant; expert tracker; weapons expert

HOMEWORLD/DIMENSION
Earth-19

WEAKNESSES
Losing powers due to old age

Gypsy's father was less understanding than his daughter. He wanted Vibe dead but soon grew to respect him when he realized that Cisco would do anything for his friends.

NAME
BREACHER

The Tales of H. R. Wells

CHAPTER 4

The cards were stacked against him, but that was nothing new for H. R. Wells. He flexed against the ropes around his wrists. They didn't budge. This mystery woman had made sure he was tied securely to the chair while he was unconscious. He peered across the room at the young woman in the rather tight-fitting blouse and jeans. She smiled, yet kept the gun trained on him.

"You didn't think I'd find you so soon, did you, Wells?" she hissed through parted teeth.

"No, I didn't, Miss . . . ?"

"Miss Take is the name," said the woman as she sauntered over toward his chair. "And I'll be your final one."

H.R. steeled himself for the coming bullet. He wrenched his eyes shut and thought about Virginia. What was she doing back home at their mountaintop farm? Why had he ever left her? Why—

Suddenly, a shot rang out.

An excerpt from one of H.R.'s books. I'm not sure writing was his thing. Come to think of it, I'm not really sure he had a thing.

When you get a bad guy who looks like a pirate, it's best just to go with it. H.R. came up with the nickname Plunder for Central City's newest jewelry thief, and let's just say the name stuck.

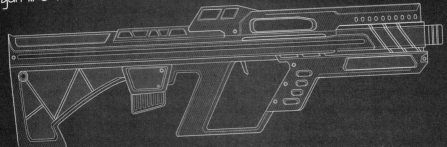

I know I got in trouble originally for making Captain Cold's gun, but man, oh man, I think it might be worth a month in the Pipeline for a gun like this one. Just from a preliminary pass, this thing can:

· Fire concussive pulses
· Shoot rapid-fire lasers
· Fire plasma cannon blasts
· Shoot heat-seeking bullets
· Fire explosive shells
· Target and fire remotely

I'm gonna take another few hours and play with . . . er . . . study it further. It could totally lead to a major breakthrough for us. Or a hole in the Speed Lab wall. Definitely one of those two. —Cisco

STR •••

ALIAS
Jared Morillo

POWERS/ABILITIES
Possesses highly advanced gun; expert marksman; expert motorcycle driver; advanced hand-to-hand combatant

HOMEWORLD/DIMENSION
Earth-1

WEAKNESSES
Susceptible to conventional attacks when unprepared or outmaneuvered

Kid Flash took Plunder down twice. We're just hoping he stays in jail this time.

NAME
PLUNDER

What is it about the future that makes everyone there want to kill me? That was the case with Abra Kadabra, a time traveler from the 64th century.

STR

ALIAS
No known alias

POWERS/ABILITIES
Utilizes 64th-century technology to appear to have almost magical abilities; body laced with nanotechnology; able to teleport, use telekinesis, conjure water, project holograms, and control various objects

HOMEWORLD/DIMENSION
Earth-1

WEAKNESSES
Power-dampening tech

NAME
ABRA KADABRA

Kadabra robbed both Stagg Industries and Kord Industries to steal parts to cobble together a time machine. We were able to stop him before he could return to his future, but something he said put an idea into my head that I just couldn't shake.

Not sure where the tabloids get their information (I should really talk to Cisco about that), but they were pretty close to the truth on this one. Kadabra being in our time gave me the idea that the only way to find out more about the mysterious Savitar who had controlled Dr. Alchemy, was to travel to the future where his identity might be common knowledge. So that's what I did. I didn't learn his name, but I learned another: Tracy Brand, the only person to ever stop Savitar.

FLASH TO THE FUTURE?

By Regal Simonson

CENTRAL CITY –
Most people believe that time travel is simply the stuff of science fiction and badly written cartoon shows, but we here at *The National Whisper* have heard otherwise. In fact, we've learned that the future was the recent vacation destination for Central City's famous Scarlet Speedster, otherwise known as the Flash.

While it's highly plausible that the Flash's trip was more business than pleasure, our sources in the metahuman community have indicated that the Fastest Man Alive may have journeyed as far forward as 2024. Is the hero simply doing a bit of sightseeing, or is he attempting to learn a bit about his own future? Or maybe he's simply trying to hit it big by finding out the winning Pick-5 numbers. In this case more than any other, only *time* will tell.

When I first met Savitar, he claimed he was a speed god. With all that armor, he almost had me convinced. However, the truth was even stranger than the fiction he presented.

STR

ALIAS
Bartholomew Henry "Barry" Allen (Time Remnant)

POWERS/ABILITIES
Superhuman speeds; super-fast healing; creates tornados or other cyclones by moving his limbs at super-speed; vibrates through solid objects; able to increase speed in others; runs so fast he can time travel; genius-level intellect; highly trained police forensic scientist; access to the geniuses at STAR Labs and its scientific equipment and weaponry; wears powerful armor that enhances his strength, power, durability, and agility; advanced knowledge of the future

HOMEWORLD/DIMENSION
Earth-1

WEAKNESSES
Mentally unstable; vulnerable to Time Wraiths like any speedster

NAME
SAVITAR

Once we realized Savitar and Dr. Alchemy were connected, I threw Alchemy's Philosopher's Stone into the Speed Force. As a result, I was shot forward in time to Infantino Street, where I witnessed Iris being murdered by Savitar in the future.

While Savitar's armor makes the perfect protective shell for a speedster, it can also operate independently from him, attacking opponents even when Savitar isn't wearing it.

STR

ALIAS
No known alias

POWERS/ABILITIES
Genius-level intellect; innovative engineer and inventor

HOMEWORLD/DIMENSION
Earth-1

WEAKNESSES
Susceptible to conventional attacks

NAME

DR. TRACY BRAND

My future self from 2024 told me that Dr. Tracy Brand was the person who devised a trap for Savitar four years after Iris was killed. So all Team Flash had to do was locate Tracy in the present and help jump-start her design—her so-called Speed Bazooka—a few years early.

Because Iris's life depended on it.

What we didn't realize was that Savitar was trapped in the Speed Force, so we essentially gave him what he wanted: the Philosopher's Stone. He was freed, and Jay Garrick later took his place in the speed prison, so as to keep the Speed Force balanced and stable.

It seemed the future I glimpsed into on Infantino Street was going to happen no matter what we did.

Savitar was a time remnant of me, a duplicate created by the Flash of 2024 to battle the future Savitar. Scarred and shunned, the time remnant decided to become Savitar to ensure that he was born in the first place.

STR

ALIAS
Lucious Coolidge

POWERS/ABILITIES
Pyromaniac who uses high-powered flamethrower to set his fires

HOMEWORLD/DIMENSION
Earth-1

WEAKNESSES
Susceptible to conventional attacks when unprepared

When we found out that Savitar had all of my memories, Cisco attempted to erase my short-term memories for a while—but he accidentally gave me complete memory loss. Unfortunately, I had to testify at the Heatmonger's trial, and because I botched it, a criminal was set free.

NAME
HEATMONGER

Luckily, I stopped the villain when I regained my memories. Now, we could once again concentrate on Savitar.

When the Speed Bazooka failed thanks to the power of the Philosopher's Stone, H. R. Wells used identity-masking technology to masquerade as Iris. He tricked Savitar into killing him, and the real Iris survived.

H.R.'s sacrifice didn't go unnoticed. Iris and I do our best every day to make the most of the future he gave us.

The future happened the way I saw it. I just didn't see it correctly the first time.

Just like that, Savitar's future never happened. The future Flash was never devastated by the death of Iris West, meaning time remnants were never created by that Flash, meaning Savitar never existed.

After one failed last-ditch effort to become a god, foiled in part by the return of Jay Garrick, Savitar eventually faded away into nothing. It was finally over.

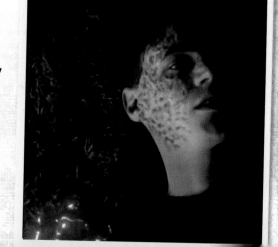

The Speed Force had become unstable. Its prison, used first to house Savitar and then to cage Jay Garrick, now needed an occupant. The only solution was for me to run into it. To save Central City from destruction, I had to sacrifice myself.

STR

ALIAS
No known alias

POWERS/ABILITIES
Robot capable of near-perfectly executed computerized hand-to-hand combat; can fire extremely powerful pulse blasts; flight; able to communicate with and monitor its subjects

HOMEWORLD/DIMENSION
Earth-1

WEAKNESSES
Can be incapacitated by significant force

NAME
SAMUROID

CENTRAL CITY POLICE DEPARTMENT
SECURITY FOOTAGE

Terrorizing the city in the hopes of fighting the Flash, the Samuroid was controlled remotely by an unknown criminal. However, its reign of terror inspired Cisco to place a quark sphere filled with my unique genetic marker in the Speed Force, effectively tricking the Speed Force into thinking it was still caging a speedster. I was freed, but I wasn't quite myself.

When I sped out of the Speed Force, a city bus was hit with a wave of dark matter. None of us had any idea at the time how important this moment was.

I have no memory of any of this, but apparently when I was freed, I was talking gibberish. The language I wrote was even stranger.

But, like she always does, Iris snapped me back to reality. When the Samuroid kidnapped her, I had no choice but to save her life.

Iris grounded me, like a lightning rod.

And the Flash was back.

Of course, coming back gave Cisco an excuse to make a new Flash suit. He tricked this one out, so I would be prepared for any situation that could crop up.

And many, many situations that would never happen.

To anyone. Ever.

ITEM	FLASH SUIT 3.0		
SCHEMATIC	CISCO RAMON	NUMBER 723	

Okay, people. The moment has arrived. Sit back, because I've outdone myself with this one:

Self-repairing armor

Nano-liquid circuitry

Deadlock system makes it so a villain can't take off the costume when Flash is unconscious

Custom-made hood loaded with maps, schematics, and even delivery take-out menus. I mean, as long as he's out, he can grab us some fried rice, right?

Babel Protocol-self-destruct sequence (I may not have thought this one through . . .)

Palms shoot concussive blasts

Flotation system inflates entire suit

Full-spectrum scanning

ALIAS
Clifford DeVoe

POWERS/ABILITIES
Genius-level intellect accelerated by his Thinking Cap; expert historian; brilliant strategist; able to absorb the bodies and/or powers of those metahumans he engineered through the dark-matter bus explosion; equipped with hi-tech hovering chair; utilizes hidden pocket dimension as headquarters

HOMEWORLD/DIMENSION
Earth-1

WEAKNESSES
Original form suffered from body degeneration due to amyotrophic lateral sclerosis; unstable mind; gives those around him no reason to trust him

NAME

THE THINKER

What I didn't realize was that the Samuroid and the dark-matter explosion that rocked a city bus were both parts of a plot engineered by Clifford DeVoe, a metahuman mastermind called the Thinker.

Clifford DeVoe was a college professor who developed a "Thinking Cap" to increase his intelligence. When the particle accelerator exploded, dark matter charged his helmet, giving him powers beyond his wildest dreams.

DeVoe was always thinking twelve steps ahead of us at every turn. For example, every victim on that bus hit with dark matter served a purpose in his plans. Each was granted a unique ability that he then absorbed like some sort of bizarre metahuman vampire, slowly becoming more and more powerful with each new body he adopted.

There were twelve people on the bus who were affected by the dark-matter wave from the Speed Force. Twelve new metahumans loose in Central City. And most of them had no intention of using their newfound abilities for good.

STR ●●●

ALIAS
Ramsey Deacon

POWERS/ABILITIES
Able to interface with anything electronic and manipulate it; expert computer programmer and hacker; genius-level intellect

HOMEWORLD/DIMENSION
Earth-1

WEAKNESSES
Cutting the power to nearby electronics renders him powerless; susceptible to computer viruses

NAME
KILG%RE

Ramsey was out for revenge against his former business partners who made a fortune from tech he designed. When we fought, he hacked his way into my suit before Iris convinced me to short out its electronics and best Kilg%re the low-tech way.

ALIAS
Becky Sharpe

POWERS/ABILITIES
Generates good luck for herself
and bad luck for others

HOMEWORLD/DIMENSION
Earth-1

WEAKNESSES
Powers can grow out of her control

Becky Sharpe had lived an
unlucky life, so it was hard
to blame her when she used
her new dark-matter powers
for her own good fortune.
But as her powers grew,
she shorted them out when
she accidentally powered
up the STAR Labs particle
accelerator.

NAME

HAZARD

ALIAS
No known alias

POWERS/ABILITIES
Emits tears that act like a
psycho-active drug

HOMEWORLD/DIMENSION
Earth-1

WEAKNESSES
Susceptible to conventional attacks

Weeper's tears are so
powerful, they could be
used as a drug to alter the
emotions of others. The
Thinker even used Weeper's
tears on his own wife when
she doubted his methods.

NAME

WEEPER

STR •••

ALIAS
Mina Chaytan

POWERS/ABILITIES
Able to temporarily bring to life inanimate objects; intelligent and extremely passionate about her cause

HOMEWORLD/DIMENSION
Earth-1

WEAKNESSES
Power-dampening technology nullifies her abilities

NAME
BLACK BISON

An extreme activist for Native American causes, Black Bison upped her game when she developed the ability to bring inanimate objects to life. It took plenty of coordination inside Team Flash to see her sentenced to Iron Heights Prison.

STR •••

ALIAS
Dominic Lanse

POWERS/ABILITIES
Advanced telepathy, including memory alteration

HOMEWORLD/DIMENSION
Earth-1

WEAKNESSES
Can manipulate minds of only those he can see

NAME
BRAINSTORM

The Thinker used Dominic to literally be in two places at once. How can you beat an enemy when you don't even know what body he's in?

ALIAS
Neil Borman

POWERS/ABILITIES
Body generates radiation that can render those within his vicinity unconscious or dead; can fire radiation blasts from his hands

HOMEWORLD/DIMENSION
Earth-1

WEAKNESSES
Unable to precisely control his powers

STR

We were only able to stop Fallout from hurting others with his radiation by using Vibe's dimensional powers to send the energy to the wasteland of Earth-15.

NAME
FALLOUT

STR

ALIAS
Sylbert Rundine

POWERS/ABILITIES
Alters the physical size of objects, humans, and animals; can both shrink and enlarge his targets; capable hand-to-hand combatant and marksman

HOMEWORLD/DIMENSION
Earth-1

WEAKNESSES
Can be incapacitated by the B.O.O.T.

A hardened killer and a collector of items he shrinks, Dwarfstar refused to answer for all of his crimes, preferring to let others take the fall for him if at all possible.

NAME
DWARFSTAR

ALIAS
Izzy Bowin

POWERS/ABILITIES
Fires powerful sound waves
from her violin or her body;
can emit a sonic scream

HOMEWORLD/DIMENSION
Earth-1

WEAKNESSES
Susceptible to conventional
attacks when unprepared

We tried to train the
Fiddler to better use her
powers, but the Thinker
got to her anyway. We
seemed to lose ground with
every new metahuman
who emerged.

NAME

FIDDLER

ALIAS
Matthew Kim

POWERS/ABILITIES
Can drain the powers of a
metahuman and transfer
them to someone else

HOMEWORLD/DIMENSION
Earth-1

WEAKNESSES
Cannot fully control powers;
must be touching victims to
transfer their abilities

Thanks to Melting Point,
Iris got to experience life
as a speedster when he
temporarily stole my powers
and gave them to her.

NAME

MELTING POINT

ALIAS
Janet Petty

POWERS/ABILITIES
Expert thief; can manipulate gravity
by touch, making objects or people
heavier or lighter

HOMEWORLD/DIMENSION
Earth-1

WEAKNESSES
Susceptible to conventional
attacks when unprepared

With a single touch, Null turned
me into a human balloon,
requiring anything but a
conventional method to save my
life. Thankfully, Team Flash is
known to be unconventional from
time to time.

NAME
NULL

ALIAS
Edwin Gauss

POWERS/ABILITIES
Able to create portals to
pocket dimensions

HOMEWORLD/DIMENSION
Earth-1

WEAKNESSES
Susceptible to conventional
attacks when unprepared

The final bus metahuman
turned out to be an . . .
interesting guy. When
not relaxing at the hippie
commune, he could "fold"
himself into a pocket
dimension at will.

NAME
FOLDED MAN

When I proposed to Iris the second time—yeah, I kinda screwed up the first go round—I made sure it was perfect. I even sang a song for her. And you know I don't bring out these pipes for just anybody.

We asked Supergirl to sing at our wedding. And in hindsight, it was a really good thing she was there . . .

Kindly Reply

KARA DANVERS & MON-EL

___ ACCEPTS WITH PLEASURE

___ DECLINES WITH REGRETS

PLEASE INDICATE ENTRÉE CHOICE

The rehearsal party was at Jitters, of course. A great night with great friends from this dimension and others.

It's not a true superhero wedding unless Nazis from the previously unknown dimension of Earth-X crash the festivities looking to murder Supergirl and give her heart to her doppelgänger, Overgirl. Now I'm not saying we outright trounced these guys, but you don't see any of us wearing evil armbands, do you?

When the smoke cleared, Iris and I decided we didn't need all the fanfare and production of a giant wedding. We just needed each other.

We got married in the park thanks to officiant John Diggle, with Oliver and Felicity serving as our witnesses and the Best Man and the Maid of Honor.

Ollie and Felicity liked the idea so much, they decided to get married right then and there, too. I've had a lot of villains try to steal my lightning over the years, but this is the first time a friend tried to steal my thunder.

I kid. I kid. Kind of.

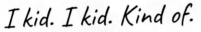

ARREST/DISPOSITION REPORT

CASE NO: CCIC:FL340

DEFENDENT IDENTIFICATION

NAME: LAST **Allen** | FIRST **Barry**

STREET ADDRESS: **4 Kanigher Plaza, Apt. 56** | CITY **Central City** | ZIP **74912**

PHONE NUMBER: ██████████ | SOCIAL SECURITY NUMBER: ██████████ | DRIVERS LICENSE: ██████████

EMPLOYER/OCCUPATION:
Central City Police Department

SEX: **Male** | RACE: **White** | DATE OF BIRTH: **3/14/1989**

HAIR: **Brown** | EYES: **Blue** | WEIGHT: **165Lbs** | HEIGHT: **6' 2"**

ARREST INFORMATION

PLACE OF ARREST:
Barry Allen's apartment

ARRESTING OFFICER: **Captain David Singh** | DATE OF ARREST: **12/24** | CHARGE DESCRIPTION: **First-Degree Murder**

FACTS OF ARREST

Suspect was found standing over the body of the deceased, Clifford DeVoe, with the murder weapon—a cake knife—nearby. The knife was covered in the victim's blood and had the suspect's prints on its handle. The suspect could offer no alibi or explanation.

RIGHT THUMBPRINT

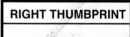

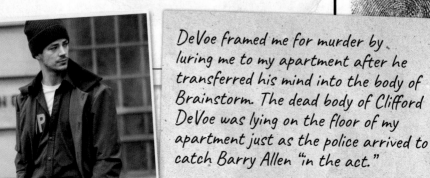

DeVoe framed me for murder by luring me to my apartment after he transferred his mind into the body of Brainstorm. The dead body of Clifford DeVoe was lying on the floor of my apartment just as the police arrived to catch Barry Allen "in the act."

As fate would have it, when I was found guilty for "killing" DeVoe, I was sentenced to the very same jail cell in Iron Heights that my father used to occupy. Guess the place is an Allen family tradition.

ALIAS
David Ratchet

ABILITIES
Bulky and strong; in prime physical condition

HOMEWORLD/DIMENSION
Earth-1

WEAKNESSES
Susceptible to conventional attacks when unprepared

NAME

BIG SIR

My dad saved Big Sir's life back when he was in Iron Heights, so Big Sir returned the favor when I rubbed some inmates the wrong way. While I couldn't officially prove that he was unjustly imprisoned for a crime that Dwarfstar actually committed, I could use my super-speed to rush him out of Iron Heights to freedom.

Looks like the movies are right. Prisons are as corrupt as they say. Take Warden Gregory Wolfe's Iron Heights for example. He was selling off the prisoners of his metahuman Meta-Block wing to the highest bidder. In this case, that bidder was underworld boss Amunet Black.

STR

ALIAS
No known alias

ABILITIES
Highly connected in the political and criminal worlds; runs Iron Heights Prison

HOMEWORLD/DIMENSION
Earth-1

WEAKNESSES
Susceptible to conventional attacks

NAME
GREGORY WOLFE

CENTRAL CITY POLICE DEPAR
SECURITY FOOTA

Wolfe didn't live long enough to sell his metahumans to Amunet. The Thinker killed him when he stormed the prison, ready to take back his dark-matter creations.

ALIAS
Leslie Jocoy

POWERS/ABILITIES
Magnetic powers enable her to use shrapnel as bullets; often forms protective metal gauntlet of scrap metal around her hand; extremely well-connected in the criminal underworld

HOMEWORLD/DIMENSION
Earth-1

WEAKNESSES
Powers can be overridden by a more powerful magnet; must have metal around her to use powers

NAME
AMUNET BLACK

Amunet has her metal-covered hands dipped into any kind of crime she can find in Central City. Most recently, she kidnapped the Weeper and sold his tears as a designer drug.

Gregory Wolfe's Meta-Block, a maximum-security containment wing at Iron Heights, intended for metahuman prisoners. But in reality, it served as Wolfe's twisted auction house.

ALIAS
Ralph Dibny

POWERS/ABILITIES
Can stretch his body to extensive lengths; able to shape-shift into objects and other humans and mimic their features and voices perfectly; capable hand-to-hand combatant; expert detective with police training; capable marksman

HOMEWORLD/DIMENSION
Earth-1

WEAKNESSES
Has a tendency not to take matters seriously

NAME

ELONGATED MAN

Out of all the people on the bus the day the Thinker engineered their dark-matter exposure, only one became a true ally of STAR Labs, and even a friend. I had known Ralph Dibny since my early days on the force. We didn't get along, and he was fired when he was caught falsifying evidence.

The dark matter not only gave Ralph powers, allowing him to become the Elongated Man, but it also helped jump-start his new life as a hero, making up for his past.

That first suit was a real stinker, Cisco. Sure, it's great it can stretch with me, but how about something with a little style, a little pizzazz. Also, pocket-sized, because I'm not one of those guys who's gonna wear his super-suit under his clothes.

Who does that? That's as silly as hiding your secret identity with, like, a pair of reading glasses or something. —Ralph

Should you tell him, or should I?

For all his nonsense—and where Ralph is concerned there's always nonsense—Ralph became a valuable member of Team Flash. His shape-shifting skills got so good he was able to impersonate Clifford DeVoe flawlessly at my appeal. With DeVoe proved to be alive, they had no choice but to let me go free.

I was finally able to concentrate on what needed to be done:

Namely, stopping the Thinker and saving my city.

But beating the Thinker didn't prove as easy as I'd hoped. DeVoe's plan was so intricate that no matter what we did, all Team Flash could hope for was to keep pace with him.

One by one, the Thinker claimed the dark-matter metahumans, absorbing their powers and killing them at the same time. It was all part of his sick scheme to "save the world from technology" by eventually using satellites to remove the intelligence of Earth's inhabitants.

Nowhere did Thinker's disturbing methods hit home harder than when he absorbed and seemingly killed Ralph Dibny.

NAME

CECILE HORTON

STR

ALIAS
No known alias

POWERS/ABILITIES
Telepathic abilities (only while pregnant); access to many members of the metahuman community; highly proficient lawyer with advanced knowledge of the legal system

HOMEWORLD/DIMENSION
Earth-1

WEAKNESSES
Susceptible to conventional attacks

In a bizarre twist of fate, Joe's girlfriend Cecile had gained the ability to read minds while she was pregnant. Using the Thinker's chair, his Thinking Cap, and Cecile's powers, I was able to send my consciousness into the Thinker's mind for a final confrontation.

What I discovered inside the Thinker's head was that Ralph wasn't dead at all. DeVoe had kept him alive, forcing Ralph to wander the landscape of the Thinker's mind, eternally lost.

With a little Flash-style positive thinking, I was able to help Ralph reclaim his body, forcing Thinker out forever. Back in the real world, we stopped DeVoe's satellites, effectively thwarting his plans. And as happy as I was to use the word "thwart" in real life, I was even happier to learn that while we were out satellite punching, Cecile and Joe had their baby, a little girl named Jenna West.

Things had finally slowed down, but that's never a permanent state of things for a Flash. Some enigmatic hero had helped me stop one of the Thinker's satellites. I thought finding out who she was would solve that particular mystery. But instead, it only deepened it.

Because when she showed up on my doorstep, she introduced herself as Nora Allen.

My daughter.
From the future . . .

So that's it. Now you're up to speed.

But my mission as the Flash isn't over. Not by a long shot. It's gone by so quickly, it feels like I'm just getting started. As long as there are Rogues robbing banks, as long as there are metahumans abusing their talents, and as long as there are people who continue to take their anger out on the world, I'll be a few seconds away, ready to run headfirst into the action with my team.

Because my name is Barry Allen. I'm the Fastest Man Alive. Try to keep up.
—The Flash

Episode Guide

Season One

S1E1: "Pilot"

After witnessing the death of his mother as a child when a bizarre yellow-and-red lightning-like figure shoots through his house one night, Barry Allen grows up to become a forensic scientist for the Central City Police Department, working closely with his adoptive father, Detective Joe West. While in his lab late one night dealing with the investigation of a killer named Clyde Mardon as well as working on his mother's own cold case, Barry Allen is struck by lightning due to a storm created during the STAR Labs particle accelerator explosion. Waking from a coma after nine months, Barry discovers he has su-

per-speed. Thanks to the staff at STAR Labs, including Dr. Harrison Wells, Dr. Caitlin Snow, and Cisco Ramon, Barry becomes Central City's superhero, dubbed the Flash by the Starling City vigilante known as the Arrow. He uses his abilities to defeat Clyde Mardon, a weather-altering villain who was also gifted powers during the particle accelerator explosion, but in the process reveals his powers to Joe West. Meanwhile, we learn about Barry's crush on his lifelong friend, Iris West, and about her current boyfriend, Joe's partner, Detective Eddie Thawne. Note: *Arrow*, Season 2, Episodes 8 and 9 take place during the beginning of this episode, when Barry travels to Starling City before the particle accelerator explosion. There he meets the Arrow and his partner Felicity Smoak, and even helps Team Arrow while they're battling the threat of the super-strong villain named Cyrus Gold.

S1E2: "Fastest Man Alive"

When he becomes faint while trying to prevent a robbery, Barry discovers that his new enhanced metabolism requires him to take in an extreme amount of calories. Meanwhile, a new criminal named Danton Black, aka Multiplex, attempts to murder millionaire industrialist Simon Stagg. While Flash successfully stops Multiplex, Stagg is murdered nonetheless, an act committed by Barry's supposed ally, Harrison Wells.

S1E3: "Things You Can't Outrun"

A new villain dubbed the Mist is killing off mobsters in Central City. When he targets Detective Joe West, Barry is forced to confront the villain in Iron Heights, eventually defeating him on a city street by overtaxing the villain's powers. Wells opts to customize metahuman jail cells out of STAR Labs' particle accelerator's cavities, a makeshift prison that soon cages the Mist. However, dealing with the accelerator forces Caitlin to relive old memories of losing her fiancé, Ronnie Raymond, in the explosion.

S1E4: "Going Rogue"

Felicity Smoak travels from Starling City to visit Barry, only to find the Flash busy dealing with Captain Cold. After Cold acquires a cryonic gun originally stolen from STAR Labs, he manages to elude capture, despite facing the Flash head-on. Meanwhile, Barry and Felicity acknowledge their flirtatious relationship, going on a double date to Jitters' trivia night with the true object of Barry's affection, Iris West, and her boyfriend, Eddie Thawne. When the Flash next fights Captain Cold, the villain gets the better of the Flash, but is later forced into a standoff with Cisco, eventually walking away from the fight. Later, Cold recruits his old partner, Mick Rory, for his next crime spree, arming him with a Heat Gun.

S1E5: "Plastique"

Barry befriends fellow particle accelerator metahuman Plastique when he learns of her explosive touch. Hunted by General Wade Eiling, Plastique eventually attempts to kill her pursuer but is shot in the process. She becomes unstable and is rushed by the Flash over the river, where she explodes. In a flashback sequence, it's revealed that Eiling and Wells have a past history, one involving the test subject Gorilla Grodd.

S1E6: "The Flash is Born"

When Barry's childhood bully is revealed as the metahuman Girder, the Flash is forced to save Iris West from the villain's clutches. Afterward, Iris writes about the superhero in her blog, dubbing him the "Flash" thanks to Barry's suggestion. Meanwhile, Joe West is looking into the murder of Barry's mother, and receives a high-velocity threat on Iris's life by a mysterious stranger.

S1E7: "Power Outage"

A charred body at a crime scene leads the Flash into a few confrontations with the new villain Blackout. When Dr. Wells frees Girder to serve as a distraction against Blackout's attack on STAR Labs, Blackout kills Girder and later overdoses on the Flash's powers and dies. Meanwhile, Clock King creates a hostage situation at Central City Police Station, until Iris saves the day. All the while, Wells continues to keep tabs on Barry Allen's future, mysteriously scheming to help the speedster.

S1E8: "Flash vs. Arrow"

The Arrow teams with Flash to help him take down the Rainbow Raider; however, their team-up becomes dysfunctional when the Raider brings out Flash's inner rage. As a result, Eddie Thawne is given the reins to an anti-Flash task force, despite Harrison Wells returning Flash to his usual heroic self. Note: The Flash heads off to Starling City to battle Captain Boomerang in *Arrow*, Season 3, Episode 8, "The Brave and the Bold."

S1E9: "The Man in the Yellow Suit"

The man responsible for Nora Allen's murder, the Reverse-Flash, rears his ugly head in Central City, attempting to steal tachyon technology from one of STAR Labs' rivals, Mercury Labs. While the Reverse-Flash easily bests Flash, the speedster nevertheless sets an ineffectual trap for the villain. With the help of the newly emerged hero Firestorm, who is revealed to be the surviving Ronnie Raymond, Flash fends off the Reverse-Flash, yet the villain escapes with the tachyon device. While his secret is still safe from the Flash, Harrison Wells later enters his Time Vault, revealing his Reverse-Flash costume.

S1E10: "Revenge of the Rogues"

Captain Cold and Heat Wave (Mick Rory) kidnap Caitlin Snow to attract the Flash's attention. Flash tricks the two villains into crossing their streams, an action that damages their weapons. They're arrested, but then are broken out of their prison transport by Captain Cold's sister, Lisa Snart. In his personal life, Barry Allen is saddened when Iris West moves in with her boyfriend, Eddie Thawne, despite Barry revealing his feelings to her in the previous episode. As a result, Barry decides to move back in with Joe West.

S1E11: "The Sound and the Fury"

After the Flash stops a few members of the Royal Flush Gang, former STAR Labs employee Hartley Rathaway, aka the Pied Piper, begins attacking his family businesses by using sonic weaponry. He is captured thanks to Wells's technology, but not before he reveals to Cisco that Harrison knew in advance that the particle accelerator could explode if activated. Meanwhile, Iris gets a job at *Central City Picture News* as a reporter, thanks to her blog about the Flash.

S1E12: "Crazy for You"

Teleporting villain Peek-a-Boo breaks into Iron Heights Prison to rescue her boyfriend, Clay Parker. Flash defeats her by trapping her in a tunnel where her vision-based powers can't function. Back at STAR Labs, Pied Piper reveals to Cisco that Firestorm is actually the merged form of both Ronnie Raymond and Dr. Professor Stein, before eluding his custody. Barry begins dating reporter Linda Park, and Central City workers are attacked by the mysterious Gorilla Grodd.

S1E13: "The Nuclear Man"

Joe West continues to investigate the cold case murder of Nora Allen, now employing Cisco's help. Visiting Barry's childhood home, they discover blood samples from two different individuals. While the blood doesn't match Wells's own, one does match that of an adult Barry Allen. Meanwhile, the STAR team tries to separate Firestorm, an act that alerts General Eiling.

S1EP14: "Fallout"

When Eiling gets his hands on Martin Stein, Ronnie Raymond and Flash are forced to rescue him, resulting in Firestorm merging once more. Firestorm decides to leave Central City in order to avoid Eiling's clutches. Angry at his interference, Reverse-Flash kidnaps Eiling and hands him over to Gorilla Grodd. At *Picture News*, Iris learns that her colleague, Mason Bridge, believes that Wells caused the particle accelerator accident on purpose.

S1EP15: "Out of Time"

Suspicious of Harrison Wells's behavior, Cisco investigates, discovering that Wells is indeed the Reverse-Flash, a man from the future named Eobard Thawne. Wells kills Cisco while the Flash is busy fighting the Weather Wizard, the revenge-seeking brother of Clyde Mardon. Before facing almost certain death, Flash reveals his identity and feelings for Iris, who realizes she also loves him. Racing faster than ever before to stop Mardon's manufactured tsunami, Flash ends up running through time into the past, stopping a day before he even started.

S1EP16: "Rogue Time"

Now aware of what's to come, Flash quickly captures the Weather Wizard. However, Captain Cold and Heat Wave return to Central City, kidnapping Cisco and forcing him to build a gun for Cold's sister, Lisa, whom Cisco later dubs the Golden Glider. Cisco is forced to reveal Barry's secret identity to Cold, causing the Flash and Captain Cold to forge an uneasy alliance. Meanwhile, Reverse-Flash kills Mason Bridge to halt his investigation.

S1EP17: "Tricksters"

A new villain adopts the name of a classic Central City foe, the Trickster. After the original Trickster escapes from Iron Heights, Flash soon discovers the two are working together to rob a reelection fundraiser for Mayor Anthony Bellows. Flash defeats the pair by learning to vibrate his molecules through solid objects. In his personal life, Barry reveals his secret identity to Eddie Thawne as he and Joe West continue to investigate the Reverse-Flash case. In a flashback sequence, it's revealed that the Reverse-Flash has been impersonating Wells after killing both Harrison and his wife years ago.

S1EP18: "All Star Team-Up"

Felicity Smoak and Ray Palmer, also known as the superhero called the Atom, arrive in Central City to get a bit of STAR Labs–style help for Ray's supersuit. Their visit turns into a team-up when the Bug-Eyed Bandit begins killing former coworkers with robotic bees. With Felicity's remote help in shutting down the bees, Flash stops the villain. Back at STAR Labs, Barry tells Cisco and Caitlin that Wells is really the Reverse-Flash. Cisco quickly believes his friend, as he is secretly experiencing memory-like flashes from the alternate timeline of Episode 15.

S1EP19: "Who Is Harrison Wells?"

As Barry and Eddie hunt down a new shape-shift-ing villain called Everyman, Eddie is framed for murder when Everyman usurps his appearance. Thanks to a serum developed by Caitlin, Flash suppresses Everyman's powers and bests him, caging him in the Pipeline holding cells and clearing Eddie Thawne's name in the process. Meanwhile, Cisco and Joe head to Starling City to investigate Harrison's past. They discover that the real Wells is dead and that their Wells is an imposter. After Cisco helps the Black Canary by designing her a sonic scream device he calls the Canary Cry, the STAR Labs team uncovers the Reverse-Flash's secret Time Vault.

S1EP20: "The Trap"

With the help of Reverse-Flash's artificial in-telligence Gideon, Barry learns of his future as the Flash and his rivalry with the Reverse-Flash. Team Flash gains more proof when Cisco uses new goggles to peer into the alternate timeline and witness his murder at Wells's hands. The Flash soon sets a trap for the Reverse-Flash, in the hopes of getting him to confess to the murder of Nora Allen, an admission that would exonerate

Barry's dad, Henry. However, when Joe West shoots and kills the Reverse-Flash, the villain is revealed as Everyman. The Reverse-Flash manages to kidnap Eddie, but perhaps most shockingly, Iris West finally deduces the Flash's secret identity.

S1EP21: "Grodd Lives"

Despite having his personal life turned upside down when Iris confronts him about being the Flash, Barry is forced to battle Gorilla Grodd. Grodd successfully kidnaps Joe West when he, Barry, and Cisco confront the monstrous beast. However, the Flash is able to battle through Grodd's psychic attacks and manages to trick Grodd into leaping in front of a subway train, thanks to Iris's coaching in his earpiece. Meanwhile, Reverse-Flash continues to build a device that will return him to his own future time period.

S1EP22: "Rogue Air"

As Reverse-Flash works to activate the particle accelerator once more, Team Flash realizes they need to relocate their prisoners. To do so, Flash requests the help of Captain Cold, who promptly double-crosses the hero, freeing the prisoners. As the accelerator is primed for activations, the Reverse-Flash faces off against not just Flash, but against Arrow and Firestorm as well. Together, the heroes defeat the Reverse-Flash.

S1E23: "Fast Enough"

With the Reverse-Flash caged in the Pipeline, Caitlin Snow and Ronnie Raymond take advantage of the downtime and finally get married. The Reverse-Flash convinces Barry to use their speed abilities together to form a wormhole that can send the Flash back to the time of his mother's death, and simultaneously allow the Reverse-Flash to return to his own future. Barry agrees but does not save his mother's life when he travels to the past. Instead, he simply says goodbye to his mom, before heading back to the present just in time to prevent the Reverse-Flash from leaving. Seeing no other way to rid the world of the powerful Reverse-Flash, Eddie Thawne shoots and kills himself, therefore ending his bloodline and preventing the Reverse-Flash

from ever existing. While the threat of the Reverse-Flash is indeed neutralized, the time manipulation results in a singularity that threatens all of Central City.

Season Two

S2E1 "The Man Who Saved Central City"

With Flash unable to stop the singularity single-handedly, Firestorm sacrifices himself to end the event. Dr. Stein survives, but Ronnie does not. The event has far-reaching consequences for the team, and they go their separate ways. Six months later, the Flash continues to work tirelessly to repair the destruction left in the wake of the singularity, Cisco works for Joe West at the police department, and Caitlin Snow works at Mercury Labs. When the Flash is given the key to the city for his reconstruction work, the ceremony is crashed by a new villain called the Atom-Smasher. The Atom-Smasher reveals to the Flash that he was sent by a villain called Zoom, a situation made even stranger with the arrival of a new Flash to Central City, Jay Garrick. And in an even stranger twist of fate, the Reverse-Flash left Barry a memory drive with a taped recording of the villain confessing to the murder of Nora Allen, evidence that results in Henry Allen finally gaining his freedom from prison.

S2E2: "Flash of Two Worlds"

Jay tells the reunited Team Flash that he was sent to their Earth from his own reality by the singularity six months ago. While he no longer has his super-speed powers, Jay has been tracking the members of Team Flash before revealing himself to them. He tells them he was locked in combat with an evil speedster named Zoom, and that Zoom is sending more metahumans to Barry's Earth from Garrick's so-called "Earth-2." One of those villains soon rears his ugly head in the form of the Sand Demon but is defeated by Barry after Jay teaches him how to hurl lightning bolts as the Flash. Meanwhile, Patty Spivot joins Joe West's metahuman task force.

S2E3: "Family of Rogues"

When the Golden Glider requests Flash's help with her brother, Captain Cold, Flash discovers that Cold is working with his ruthless father against his will. Snart's father had placed a bomb inside of Golden Glider and had threatened to detonate it if Captain Cold wouldn't pull off a heist with him. Going undercover as a criminal, Barry joins Snart's crew until Cisco successfully removes the bomb from Lisa. Cold then kills his father as retribution, before he's imprisoned in Iron Heights. Meanwhile, Earth-2 Harrison "Harry" Wells arrives at STAR Labs through the breach.

S2E4: "The Fury of Firestorm"

When Professor Stein proves to be in a critical, unstable condition without another half of Firestorm, Team Flash looks to find a replacement for Ronnie, ultimately settling on Jefferson Jackson, a high-school football star caught in the particle accelerator's wave of energy. He successfully merges with Stein, and helps defeat Henry Hewitt, another possible Firestorm candidate who proved mentally unstable. To make matters more complicated, a hulking metahuman monster named King Shark attacks Flash, only to be subdued by Harry Wells.

S2E5: "The Darkness and the Light"

Responsible for Earth-2's metahumans and Zoom's powers, Harry Wells sets up camp on Earth-1 to help the Flash in his efforts. Their partnership starts earlier than expected when Earth-2's Linda Park begins robbing banks in the guise of Dr. Light. Flash defeats her using a speed mirage. In their personal lives, Barry begins to date Patty Spivot, while Cisco has his eye on a barista at Jitters named Kendra Saunders. At Barry's suggestion, Cisco adopts the superhero name Vibe. Meanwhile on Earth-2, Zoom has captured Jesse, the daughter of Harry Wells.

S2E6: "Enter Zoom"

Using her powers to make herself invisible, Dr. Light escapes from her cell at STAR Labs. In an attempt to trap Zoom, Barry reveals his secret identity to Earth-1's Linda Park and has her dress like her Earth-2 doppelgänger. Zoom sees through the plot, however, injuring Barry and temporarily paralyzing him.

S2E7: "Gorilla Warfare"

Henry Allen returns to Central City to help Barry overcome his fears about facing Zoom, since Barry has fully recovered physically from his temporary paralysis. Meanwhile, Harry Wells helps rescue a kidnapped Caitlin Snow from the clutches of Gorilla Grodd. The Flash then sends Grodd to Earth-2 to a jungle sanctuary called Gorilla City. In his personal life, Cisco uses his powers to "vibe" Kendra, seeing her as a winged angel-like figure in his vision.

S2E8: "Legends of Today"

When the immortal villain Vandal Savage arrives in Central City searching for Kendra Saunders, Team Flash heads to Starling City to enlist the aid of Green Arrow. However, Kendra is abducted by the mysterious Hawkman, forcing a confrontation with Flash and Green Arrow. Note: In *Arrow*, Season 4, Episode 8, Savage is defeated when Flash travels back in time. In *Legends of Tomorrow*, Season 1, Episode 1, Hawkman and Hawkgirl go on to join the time traveling Legends team with other Flash supporting characters, Firestorm, Captain Cold, and Heat Wave.

S2E9: "Running to Stand Still"

Weather Wizard, Captain Cold, and the Trickster all join forces to kill the Flash. However, their schemes are foiled by Team Flash, who use the dimensional breaches to destroy Trickster's exploding Christmas gifts. Meanwhile, Joe West meets his son named Wally, and Wells agrees to work with Zoom in order to save Jesse's life.

S2E10: "Potential Energy"

The Flash faces the Turtle, a metahuman able to slow down others. After the Turtle captures Patty Spivot, Flash saves her, only to learn that Patty is leaving him and Central City behind. When the Turtle is safely imprisoned at STAR Labs, Wells kills him in order to extract a sample of his brain matter.

S2E11: "The Reverse-Flash Returns"

When Vibe detects the return of the Reverse-Flash, Flash is forced to face his old foe once more, and bests him in a battle of speed. Barry then sends Thawne to the future to save Vibe's life. Meanwhile, Iris and Wally West reconcile with their mother, Francine, as she lies on her deathbed, and Barry says goodbye to Patty, who has deduced his secret identity.

S2E12: "Fast Lane"

A product of the STAR Labs particle accelerator explosion, new villain Tar Pit emerges to wreak havoc. Flash stops him, but discovers a deadlier threat when Wells reveals he's been working for Zoom. After Flash figures out how to seal the breaches to Earth-2, he refuses to seal the final breach. Instead, he promises to save Jesse from Zoom.

S2E13: "Welcome to Earth-2"

The Flash and Vibe travel to Earth-2 where Barry impersonates his Earth-2 self to find out more about the weird dimension. They discover many differences, including Caitlin Snow's persona as Killer Frost, an evil Firestorm called Deathstorm, and Vibe's cruel doppelgänger, Reverb. Despite the Flash's best efforts, he's captured by Zoom and taken to his stronghold. Back on Earth-1, Jay Garrick confronts the villain Geomancer using a Caitlin-designed formula, Velocity-7, to temporarily increase his speed.

S2E14: "Escape from Earth-2"

On Earth-2, Wells and Cisco convince Killer
Frost to help them battle Zoom. After meeting
one of Zoom's prisoners, a mysterious man in
an iron mask, Flash and Jesse escape Zoom's
holding cell with the help of their allies. Back
on Earth-1, Caitlin develops Velocity-9 for Jay,
who uses the formula to fight Geomancer. Finally, Flash, Vibe, Jesse, and Harry Wells return
to Earth-1. Just as they close the breach behind
them, Jay is stabbed by Zoom and brought back
to Earth-2.

S2E15: "King Shark"

King Shark escapes his prison in the ARGUS
"aquarium," returning to Central City. With the
help of Green Arrow's friend John Diggle, the
Flash traps King Shark in a water vortex before
electrifying him with a lightning bolt. King Shark
is returned to ARGUS and the custody of its new
director, Lyla Michaels.

S2E16: "Trajectory"

When a Mercury Labs employee uses Velocity-9
to become a speedster and commit robberies as
Trajectory, Flash takes a break from his Zoom
training to stop the new villain. Afterward,
thanks to one of Cisco's vibes and Barry's de-
ductions, Team Flash realizes that Jay Garrick is
also Zoom himself.

S2E17: "Flash Back"

Realizing that the Reverse-Flash may have
the answers Barry seeks, the Flash travels
back in time to impersonate his past self and
learn from the imposter Harrison Wells. As the
Reverse-Flash agrees to help Flash become
faster, Barry is pursued by a Time Wraith, a
creature disturbed when speedsters mess with
the timeline. After the Reverse-Flash gives Barry
information about tachyon technology that can
increase his speed, the Flash races back to the
current timeline, narrowly avoiding the Time
Wraith with the help of the Pied Piper.

S2E18: "Versus Zoom"

It is revealed that years ago on Earth-2, Hunter Zolomon witnessed his mother's murder at the hands of his father. Hunter grows up to become a serial killer, and while being electrocuted, gains power through the Earth-2 particle accelerator explosion. In the present, Vibe opens the breach to Earth-2. After facing the Flash, Zoom kidnaps Wally West, demanding Flash trade him his enhanced speed for Wally's life. The Flash agrees to the terms, Harry Wells removes Barry's speed, and Zoom injects the speed into himself before escaping with the kidnapped Caitlin Snow.

S2E19: "Back to Normal"

Now powerless, Barry Allen is forced to fight Griffin Grey, a particle accelerator metahuman, with only the help of Team Flash and his wits. Super-strong due to his metahuman abilities, Grey also ages every time he uses his powers. Flash and his teammates battle Grey, who dies in the process. Meanwhile on Earth-2, Caitlin meets her doppelgänger Killer Frost, and helps her escape from Zoom's holding cell. Killer Frost is soon killed by Zoom, and Caitlin remains in his captivity.

S2E20: "Rupture"

With a fake Flash hologram zipping around the city to deter suspicion, Harry Wells tries to convince Barry to re-create the particle accelerator explosion to re-create his powers. Meanwhile, Zoom sends Earth-2's Rupture to police headquarters. Zoom rushes in and kills the officers and Rupture in his bid to take over Central City. Despite protests from the newly returned Henry Allen, Barry decides to re-create the particle accelerator explosion. The event catches Jesse Quick and Wally in the blast, leaving Jesse in a coma, and seemingly vaporizing Barry.

S2E21: "The Runaway Dinosaur"

Having survived the particle accelerator explosion, Barry realizes he's trapped in the Speed Force, and he must chase a moving target to regain his speed. After finally coming to terms with his mother's death, Barry is able to leave the dreamlike realm and return to Earth, his speed powers intact. No sooner does he return than he's forced to defeat the zombie version of Girder and help Jesse Quick out of her coma using his lightning.

S2E22: "Invincible"

Having compiled an army of Earth-2 metahumans, including new faces like Black Siren, Zoom traps Central City in a Metapocalypse. Team Flash defeats the onslaught by developing a sonic amplifier that assaults beings existing on the specific vibration pattern of Earth-2 and renders them unconscious. The Flash gathers up the fallen villains, but Zoom escapes back to his world. He later returns, forcing Barry to use his powers in front of Wally West and reveal his secret. But far worse, Zoom then kills Henry Allen in front of his son.

S2E23: "The Race of His Life"

Zoom baits Barry into a race, one that will charge Zolomon's stolen Magnetar, a device capable of wiping out all life on every Earth, save for Earth-1. The Flash indeed races Zoom but creates a time remnant of himself who stops the Magnetar, sacrificing his own life in the process. Flash defeats Zoom just as Time Wraiths drag the villain away. In the aftermath, Flash frees the man in the iron mask from Zoom's holding cell on Earth-2, discovering that he is Earth-3's Flash, a doppelgänger of Henry Allen. Unable to cope with the tragedies of his life, Flash runs back in time and stops the Reverse-Flash from ever killing Nora Allen in the first place.

Season Three

S3E1: "Flashpoint"

Reality has changed now that the Flash has saved his mother's life. Back in the present, Barry discovers that both of his parents are alive and well in this new reality dubbed Flashpoint. Barry has no need to use his powers; as Kid Flash, Wally West patrols the city streets, keeping it safe from villains like the speedster Rival. When Wally is severely injured, however, Flash is forced to race back in time to reset the timeline to the way things used to be, allowing Reverse-Flash to kill his mother in the process. However, not everything remains the same.

S3E2: "Paradox"

In this newly revised reality, Cisco's brother Dante is dead, Barry has a forensics partner named Julian Albert, and Caitlin has the same powers as Killer Frost. Meanwhile, a new villain later dubbed Dr. Alchemy has the ability to unlock the powers of metahumans from the Flashpoint timeline. He does so for Rival, who is only defeated by the combined teamwork of Flash and Vibe. Now aware that changing the past is no longer the solution, Barry works on the present, and he and Iris West finally begin dating.

S3E3: "Magenta"

When Harry and Jesse Wells return to Earth-1, Jesse reveals that the particle accelerator explosion reenactment indeed gave her super powers. After Dr. Alchemy successfully unlocks the magnetic powers of Magenta, this new villain lashes out at her abusive foster father. Only by teaming with Jesse does Flash save the day, inspiring Harry to gift his daughter with her own superhero costume for her new life as Jesse Quick.

S3E4: "The New Rogues"

As revealed in a flashback, Mirror Master and his girlfriend, the Top, gain their powers during the particle accelerator explosion. Finding his way out of the mirror dimension he had been trapped in, Mirror Master teams with the Top on a crime spree. Flash and Jesse Quick confront them, only to see Flash trapped inside a mirror. After Caitlin secretly uses her cold power to break Barry free, the Flash and Jesse Quick challenge Mirror Master and the Top to a rematch and best the new Rogues. Jesse and Harry head back to Earth-2, but first, Team Flash picks a replacement Harry from Earth-19, H.R. Wells.

S3E5: "Monster"

When a literal giant monster begins causing havoc on the streets of Central City, Flash and his team look into it, eventually realizing it's just a hologram created by a misguided teenager. Meanwhile, the suspicious H. R. Wells turns out to lack scientific knowledge, and merely answered the call to live on Earth-1 to gain material for a book he's writing. Also, Caitlin's powers continue to develop, and she visits her scientist mother for help.

S3E6: "Shade"

A Flashpoint villain dubbed Shade battles and is bested by the Flash, but he's not nearly the deadliest threat the Scarlet Speedster has on his plate at the moment. Because when Dr. Alchemy successfully tempts Wally West to unlock his Kid Flash powers, Wally picks up the Philosopher's Stone, causing the young Mr. West to become encased in a bizarre cocoon. The Flash soon battles Dr. Alchemy's boss, the mysterious metal-encased speedster called Savitar.

S3E7: "Killer Frost"

When Caitlin's usual personality is overtaken by her cruel Killer Frost persona, she heads to Central City police headquarters to interrogate one of Dr. Alchemy's lackeys. Flash and Vibe confront her, only to be sent reeling when Killer Frost reveals that Barry was responsible for the death of Cisco's brother. Meanwhile, an impatient and worried Joe West breaks Wally out of his cocoon, and a regretful Caitlin works to stabilize Wally's super-fast condition. By the episode's end, it's revealed that Julian Albert and Dr. Alchemy are one and the same.

S3E8: "Invasion!"

After discovering an alien crash site, the Flash recruits Team *Arrow*, Supergirl, and the Legends to fight the oncoming threat. In a conflict that involves mind-controlled heroes and time travel to 1951, the heroes defeat the Dominator aliens by using nanotechnology. Note: This storyline ran through *Arrow*, Season 5, Episode 8, as well as *Legends of Tomorrow*, Season 2, Episode 7.

S3E9: "The Present"

The Flash and Jay Garrick team up to obtain the Philosopher's Stone from Dr. Alchemy, narrowly avoiding death by Savitar's hands. Barry soon learns that Julian is Dr. Alchemy's alter ego and reveals his own double identity to his confused lab partner. Julian reveals how he discovered the Stone, and Team Flash uses Julian to communicate with Savitar. Barry decides to throw the Philosopher's Stone into the Speed Force but is sent into the future and witnesses Iris dying at Savitar's hands. Meanwhile, Wally West is given a Kid Flash costume and Barry finds an apartment to share with Iris.

S3E10: "Borrowing Problems From the Future"

The Flash fights a new villain called Plunder, but it's Kid Flash who defeats the criminal when Barry attempts to change the future by altering some of the events scheduled to lead up to Iris's death. Meanwhile, H. R. Wells founds a STAR Labs Museum, but isn't successful until Cisco offers him a helping hand. Julian joins Team Flash, and the mysterious Gypsy shows up on Earth-1.

S3E11: "Dead or Alive"

Hailing from H.R.'s world of Earth-19, the Collector known as Gypsy is charged with finding and executing Wells for breaking their world's strict rules against dimension hopping. When Vibe sees Gypsy briefly leave herself open to attack as she teleports, he uses this flaw against her when he challenges her in a duel to the death. Vibe wins, but spares Gypsy's life. Gypsy returns to her dimension, prepared to lie and tell her superiors that H.R. is in fact dead.

S3E12: "Untouchable"

The Flash attempts to train Kid Flash, as he believes Wally to be naturally faster, and therefore able to defeat Savitar. However, first the Flash must contend with Clive Yorkin, a metahuman activated by Dr. Alchemy. Kid Flash learns how to phase through objects and phases through Clive, stopping the villain. Back at STAR Labs, Jesse Quick emerges through the portal, saying that her father has been kidnapped by Gorilla Grodd.

S3E13: "Attack on Gorilla City"

Flash, Vibe, Caitlin, and Julian head to Earth-2's Gorilla City but are captured by Gorilla Grodd and reunited with Harry Wells in the process. To win his freedom, the Flash battles Grodd's adversary, Solovar, and defeats him. However, Grodd backs out of his end of the deal, and instead takes over Gorilla City, forcing the Flash to escape by faking his own death. The heroes retreat to Earth-1; however, Grodd is hot on their trail thanks to his captive, a mind-controlled Gypsy.

S3E14: "Attack on Central City"

Grodd invades Earth-1, leading an army of intelligent gorillas. Using his powers to activate a missile launcher, Grodd nearly sends a nuclear missile toward Central City before Flash stops him by deactivating its launcher. Marching his troops on the City, Grodd is defeated when Vibe and Gypsy retrieve Solovar from Earth-2, and the gorilla bests Grodd in combat, proving himself the rightful ruler of Gorilla City. His troops obey him as he orders them to return home. Later, with the chaos over, Barry proposes to Iris.

S3E15: "The Wrath of Savitar"

After using Julian to commune with Savitar, Team Flash discovers that Caitlin has been keeping a part of the Philosopher's Stone in an attempt to cure her of her powers. Kid Flash steals the stone and hurls it into the Speed Force, not realizing that that's exactly what Savitar wants. Wally is sucked into the Speed Force, and the Flash is forced to fight off Savitar until the villain retreats for the time being.

S3E16: "Into the Speed Force"

The Flash travels into the Speed Force to save Kid Flash but can escape only when Jay Garrick sacrifices himself to fill the gap of a speedster prisoner left vacant by Savitar's escape. Meanwhile, Jesse Quick confronts Savitar, and then later decides to head to Earth-3 to protect it until Jay can return. When Barry and Iris finally get some time alone, they break up because Iris suspects Barry proposed to her only to change the timeline.

S3E17: "Duet"

When the Music Meister puts Supergirl in a coma in *Supergirl*, Season 2, Episode 16, her allies Martian Manhunter and Mon-El bring her to Earth-1. However, the Music Meister soon puts the Flash in a coma as well, and the two heroes must fight through a musical reality to regain consciousness. When Barry does return to the real world, he sings a song to propose to Iris, and she accepts.

S3E18: "Abra Kadabra"

Sixty-fourth-century supervillain Abra Kadabra begins a hi-tech crime spree, until he is captured by the Flash. However, he manages to escape custody, causing an explosion that injures Caitlin. She is forced to talk Julian through an operation to save her own life, one that triggers her evil Killer Frost personality. Meanwhile, the Flash and Gypsy defeat Kadabra after he builds a time machine, and Barry decides to travel to the future to find a way to save Iris's life from the oncoming threat of Savitar.

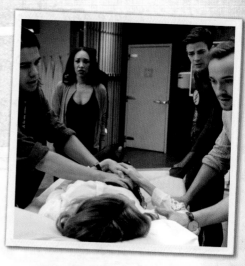

S3E19: "The Once and Future Flash"

The Flash visits a possible future of 2024, in which Team Flash has long gone their separate ways and Mirror Master and the Top run amuck. While the Flash is unable to learn Savitar's true identity as he had hoped, the future Flash tells him about Tracy Brand, a scientist who will eventually be able to trap Savitar in the Speed Force. The Flash returns to the present, unaware that Killer Frost is currently joining forces with Savitar after witnessing his true identity.

S3E20: "I Know Who You Are"

Team Flash successfully recruits Tracy Brand after saving her life from Killer Frost. Barry soon deduces that Savitar is actually an alternate version of himself, and confronts Savitar with that knowledge. Meanwhile, Joe West reveals Barry's secrets to his girlfriend, Cecile.

S3E21: "Cause and Effect"

Revealed as a corrupted time remnant of the Flash, Savitar's goal is to kill Iris West to ensure that he is created in the first place. To prevent Savitar from knowing their plan, Vibe tries to alter Flash's brain so he can't forge new memories but instead gives him complete amnesia. Barry tries to live his civilian life, and even testify against a villain called Heatmonger, but his lack of memory allows Heatmonger to walk free. Flash's memories are restored just in time to defeat Heatmonger as he starts a fire in a skyscraper. Meanwhile, Tracy not only begins a relationship with H. R. Wells but she also develops her Speed Bazooka to trap Savitar, though it requires an advanced power source.

S3E22: "Infantino Street"

With the alien power source needed to power the Speed Bazooka in an ARGUS holding cell, Flash is forced to recruit Captain Cold to help him steal the device. The two successfully steal it and defeat its unwitting guardian, King Shark, but are discovered by Lyla Michaels. She allows them to take the power source, and Team Flash constructs the bazooka. Savitar then tricks H. R. Wells to reveal the location of the hidden Iris, kidnaps her, and even fends off the attack from the Speed Bazooka. Then just as Flash saw when he traveled through time, Savitar kills Iris in front of him and escapes.

S3E23: "Finish Line"

Using a device that altered his physical appearance, H. R. Wells had switched places with Iris West. He dies as Iris reveals she is alive, and the Flash soon finds himself locked in battle with his future time remnant. Savitar plans to modify the Speed Bazooka to disperse himself throughout time, effectively becoming a god. However, Vibe instead uses the device to free Jay Garrick from the Speed Force. As Vibe convinces Killer Frost to end her partnership with Savitar, Barry beats the villain, and Savitar is erased from the timeline. After mourning the death of H.R., Barry enters the Speed Force to fill the void left by Jay, sacrificing himself to save his city.

Season Four

S4E1: "The Flash Reborn"

With Barry trapped in the Speed Force, Iris West has taken over the leadership of Team Flash. However, Vibe concocts a way to rescue Barry, just in time to face the new threat of the Samuroid. The plan works, and after a period of talking incoherently, the Flash snaps back to his regular personality when Iris places herself in danger. The Samuroid is defeated, but Team Flash has no idea that the Samuroid's creator, a new villain named the Thinker, poses much more of a threat.

S4E2: "Mixed Signals"

Flash tests out a new hi-tech costume, only to have its systems hacked by new villain Kilg%re. When Iris suggests throwing lightning at his own suit to short out the system, Flash succeeds in besting the villain and taking him to Iron Heights. However, the Flash is unaware that Kilg%re is just a small part in the Thinker's plan. Meanwhile, Team Flash suffers a bit in the relationship department as Vibe has to cancel a date with Gypsy, and Barry and Iris attend couple's counseling.

S4E3: "Luck Be a Lady"

New villain Hazard begins to use her good-luck powers to rob banks, as Team Flash discovers that she was one of twelve people exposed to dark matter when the Flash hastily exited the Speed Force. Flash manages to stop Hazard when her powers accidentally activate the particle accelerator and nullify themselves. On the personal side of things, Jesse Quick breaks up with Kid Flash and Cecile reveals that she's pregnant with Joe West's baby.

S4E4: "Elongated Journey Into Night"

While Vibe is busy fighting off Gypsy's father, an angry metahuman named Breacher, Barry reconnects with a former coworker and adversary of his, Ralph Dibny. Dibny was exposed to dark matter on the bus, and gained stretching powers. When Vibe saves Dibny's life, Breacher is impressed and lets his prey live. Ralph then joins Team Flash.

S4E5: "Girls Night Out"

Iris heads out on her bachelorette party with Caitlin, Felicity, and Cecile, while Barry enjoys a bachelor party usurped by Ralph Dibny. While Barry and his friends end up intoxicated and jailed for rowdy behavior, Iris stumbles on a plot by crime boss Amunet Black to sell the tears of a dark-matter metahuman named the Weeper as an illegal drug. The women momentarily defeat Black, but the Weeper is later captured by the Thinker.

S4E6: "When Harry Met Harry . . ."

Vibe creates a prototype suit for Ralph as the Flash begins to train the newest member of their team. However, a new dark-matter metahuman named Black Bison interrupts them by stealing Native American artifacts. Flash and Ralph defeat Bison by working together. Meanwhile, back at STAR Labs, Harry Wells calls together a Council of Wells from other realities to learn that the man who orchestrated the dark-matter bus incident, the Thinker, is really the wheel-chair-bound Clifford DeVoe.

S4E7: "Therefore I Am"

It is revealed that DeVoe was caught in the original particle accelerator explosion at STAR Labs while wearing a Thinking Cap device that increased his brain power. Later, amyotrophic lateral sclerosis caused DeVoe to become wheelchair bound. In the present day, the Flash investigates DeVoe, discovering a camera he planted inside the head of the Samuroid. He confronts the villain, who reveals his true identity and is dubbed the Thinker by Vibe.

S4E8: "Crisis on Earth-X, Part 3"

In *Supergirl*, Season 3, Episode 8, and *Arrow*, Season 6, Episode 8, a four-part crossover begins with Barry and Iris organizing their wedding. Despite a successful rehearsal dinner, the actual wedding is crashed by Nazis from the dimension known as Earth X. As Team Flash partners with Team Arrow, the Legends, and Supergirl, they eventually triumph over their evil counterparts. Note: In *Legends of Tomorrow*, Season 3, Episode 8, Barry and Iris finally tie the knot in a private ceremony officiated by John Diggle. Green Arrow and Felicity Smoak opt to get married at the same time.

S4E9: "Don't Run"

As bad luck would have it, the Thinker kidnaps the Flash just as Amunet Black kidnaps Caitlin Snow. While Black attempts to force Caitlin to operate surgically on a dark-matter metahuman called Brainstorm, the Flash escapes the Thinker's clutches. Caitlin also escapes just in time for Team Flash to celebrate the Christmas holiday. Barry leaves the party when he gets a call from the Thinker, discovering that the Thinker has transferred his own consciousness into Brainstorm, and left his deceased body in Barry's apartment in order to frame him for murder.

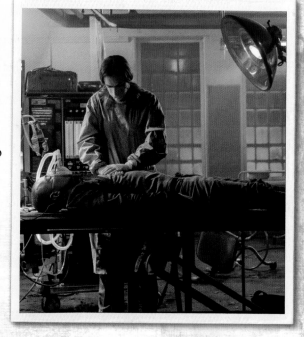

S4E10: "The Trial of the Flash"

Joe's girlfriend Cecile represents Barry Allen at his murder trial, but since he refuses to admit to the world that he's secretly the Flash, Barry is found guilty and sentenced to life in prison. Meanwhile, Team Flash tangles with dark-matter metahuman Fallout, forcing Barry to leave his own trial and use super-speed to create a vacuum around the villain while Vibe opens a portal to harmlessly drain the radiation.

S4E11: "The Elongated Knight Rises"

Occupying the same cell as his father before him, Barry befriends fellow Iron Heights inmate Big Sir. The Trickster II breaks out of the same prison thanks to the efforts of his mom, Prank, until Dibny helps Team Flash defeat them.

S4E12: "Honey, I Shrunk Team Flash"

When Dibny and Vibe face a dark-matter metahuman named Dwarfstar, he shrinks them dramatically using his powers. They later trick the villain into growing them back to regular size, and see him arrested. When Barry discovers that Dwarfstar committed the murder Big Sir was arrested for, he runs Big Sir out of prison, drawing the attention of the corrupt Warden Wolfe, who wants to sell the Flash to Amunet Black. Meanwhile, in a strange twist of fate, Cecile develops telepathic abilities as a result of her pregnancy.

S4E13: "True Colors"

With the Flash locked in the secret metahuman wing at Iron Heights, Warden Wolfe prepares to sell Barry and some dark-matter metahuman captives to Amunet Black. Flash leads a breakout but is interrupted by Black's forces and the Thinker. Before Flash can stop him, the Thinker absorbs the abilities of the dark-matter villains and transfers his consciousness into Hazard's body. However, Barry nevertheless finds himself a free man when Ralph Dibny uses his newly discovered shape-shifting abilities to impersonate DeVoe at Barry's appeal, tricking the judge into believing that DeVoe was never murdered in the first place.

S4E14: "Subject 9"

After Team Flash discovers a new dark-matter metahuman dubbed the Fiddler, the Thinker takes control of her body, besting Team Flash. In his personal life, Barry is indefinitely suspended from the Central City Police Department, due to suspicions aroused during his murder trial.

S4E15: "Enter Flashtime"

Flash uses his super-speed like never before when a villain named Veronica Cale sets in motion a nuclear bomb detonation. Moving so fast that time seems paused, Barry touches some of his allies to bring them up to his speed, eventually discovering the solution to preventing the blast thanks to Iris's advice. He temporarily removes the quark sphere—the device tricking the Speed Force into thinking it's imprisoning a speedster—sending a lightning bolt into the nuclear weapon and disarming it.

S4E16: "Run, Iris, Run"

When dark-matter metahuman Melting Point
transfers Flash's speed into Iris, Iris finally gets
a chance at being a speedster. Meanwhile, Harry
Wells develops his own Thinking Cap to use
against the Thinker, but Team Flash uses it to
defeat Melting Point. The incarcerated villain
then transfers Iris's speed back into Barry.

Episode 17: "Null and Annoyed"

When a new dark-matter villain named Null
goes on a crime spree, the Flash is forced to let
Elongated Man use his own less-than-serious
methods to save the day and capture the villain.
Meanwhile, Vibe discovers Breacher's powers
are waning due to old age, and is offered a job
as Breacher's replacement. Back at the Thinker's lair, his wife learns she is being drugged by
her husband, only to have her memory erased,
an event that has happened many times before.

S4E18: "Lose Yourself"

After meeting the final bus metahuman, the
Folded Man, the Elongated Man realizes he
can use the Folded Man's powers to teleport
into the Thinker's secret pocket dimension.
Planning to kill the villain, Ralph attacks the
Thinker, only to discover that he's been duped,
and the Thinker is raiding STAR Labs at that
exact moment. The Thinker bests Ralph and
transfers his mind into Ralph's body, using his
shape-shifting powers to shape himself into
DeVoe's original form.

S4E19: "Fury Rogue"

To keep Fallout safe from the Thinker, the Flash
enlists the help of Citizen Cold from Earth-X
on the day before Cold's wedding to the Ray.
However, Siren-X from Earth-X follows Cold
to Earth-1 and attacks the team. Flash manages
to defeat Siren-X, and Fallout is secured at a
new ARGUS location.

S4E20: "Therefore She Is"

As flashbacks reveal how the Thinker and his wife, Marlize, fell in love, the couple steal the computers needed for their Enlightenment Machine in the present day. Team Flash discovers that the Thinker's ultimate goal is to cease all technology in the world by reducing the intelligence of the entire population of the planet. Marlize eventually decides that the Thinker is too far gone to stand beside, and leaves her husband. But the villainous couple are not the only ones to part ways, as Gypsy and Vibe also decide to break up.

S4E21: "Harry and the Harrisons"

With Harry's intelligence damaged by his own Thinking Cap, Vibe recruits a Council of Harrisons to assist him. Meanwhile, the Flash seeks out Amunet Black and receives a bomb made from her metal with the capability of destroying one of the satellites the Thinker plans to employ.

S4E22: "Think Fast"

The Thinker uses his powers to invade ARGUS and charge his satellites with their prisoner, Fallout. While the Flash brings Vibe and Caitlin with him into "Flashtime" and successfully takes out one of the Thinker's satellites, DeVoe later breaks into STAR Labs and hijacks the Time Vault, using STAR's own satellite to replace the one that was destroyed. Meanwhile, Iris and Wells track down Marlize and enlist her help.

S4E23: "We Are the Flash"

Using Cecile's temporary psychic powers, the Flash enters the mind of the Thinker and discovers Ralph Dibny still alive in his consciousness. The two escape the Thinker's brain, allowing Ralph to take control of his body once more, effectively ending the Thinker in the process. After they stop the Thinker's satellites, Team Flash is overjoyed to meet the newest addition to their family, Joe and Cecile's baby, Jenna. However, another new family member introduces herself at the episode's end when Barry meets his speedster daughter from the future, Nora.

ABRAMS would like to thank the team of superheroes at Warner Bros. who helped make this book possible: Joshua Anderson, Amy Weingartner, Juli Ruiz, Catherine Shin, Greg Berlanti, Todd Helbing, Sarah Schechter, and Carl Ogawa, as well as Delia Greve and the fantastic team at Becker & Mayer.

ISBN 978-1-4197-2938-6

Text by Matthew K. Manning
Book design by Eddee Helms
Design assistance by Megan Sugiyama

Printed and bound in the USA
10 9 8 7 6 5 4 3 2 1

Amulet Books are available at special discounts when purchased in quantity for premiums and promotions as well as fundraising or educational use. Special editions can also be created to specification. For details, contact specialsales@abramsbooks.com or the address below.

Amulet Books® is a registered trademark of Harry N. Abrams, Inc.

ABRAMS The Art of Books
195 Broadway, New York, NY 10007
abramsbooks.com